"I'm trying to do the right thing here. The decent thing. You've just been through a hell of a bad time. You're scared, and you're vulnerable."

"And you felt sorry for me." Her chin came up, and she smiled. "That *is* what you're trying to say, isn't it?"

"That's just it, Stacy, I don't feel. It's the way I like it. The way it has to be."

"I think you feel very deeply. Too deeply. And I think you felt something just now when you kissed me."

He felt the heat climbing up his neck. He was immune to nearly every wile a woman possessed— everything but the unguarded look of longing in the eyes of a woman who believed in him....

Dear Reader,

There's something for everyone this month! Brides, babies and cowboys...but also humor, sensuality...and delicious love stories (some without a baby in sight!).

There's nothing as wonderful as a new book from Barbara Boswell, and this month we have a MAN OF THE MONTH written by this talented author. *Who's the Boss?* is a very sexy, delightfully funny love story. As always, Barbara not only creates a masterful hero and smart-as-a-whip heroine, she also makes her secondary characters come alive!

When a pregnant woman gets stuck in a traffic jam she does the only thing she can do—talks a handsome hunk into giving her a ride to the hospital on his motorcycle in Leanne Banks's latest, *The Troublemaker Bride*.

Have you ever wanted to marry a millionaire? Well, heroine Irish Ellison plans on finding a man with money in *One Ticket to Texas* by Jan Hudson. A single mom-to-be gets a new life in Paula Detmer Riggs's emotional and heartwarming *Daddy by Accident*. And a woman with a "bad reputation" finds unexpected romance in Barbara McMahon's *Boss Lady and the Hired Hand*.

Going to your high-school reunion is bad enough. But what if you were voted "Most likely to succeed"...but your success at love has been fleeting? Well, that's just what happens in Susan Connell's *How To Succeed at Love*.

So read...and enjoy!

*Lucia Macro*

Lucia Macro
Senior Editor

Please address questions and book requests to:
Silhouette Reader Service
U.S.: 3010 Walden Ave., P.O. Box 1325, Buffalo, NY 14269
Canadian: P.O. Box 609, Fort Erie, Ont. L2A 5X3

# PAULA
# DETMER RIGGS
# DADDY BY ACCIDENT

SILHOUETTE *Desire*®
Published by Silhouette Books
America's Publisher of Contemporary Romance

SILHOUETTE BOOKS

ISBN 0-373-76073-6

DADDY BY ACCIDENT

Copyright © 1997 by Paula Detmer Riggs

Printed in U.S.A.

---

## PAULA DETMER RIGGS

discovers material for her writing in her varied life experiences. During her first five years of marriage to a naval officer, she lived in nineteen different locations on the West Coast, gaining familiarity with places as diverse as San Diego and Seattle. While working at a historical site in San Diego she wrote, directed and narrated fashion shows and became fascinated with the early history of California.

She writes romances because "I think we all need an escape from the high-tech pressures that face us every day, and I believe in happy endings. Isn't that why we keep trying, in spite of all the roadblocks and disappointments along the way?"

For Catherine Anderson, who has a great talent, a generous heart and an astonishing wisdom. Thanks for being my friend.

# One

Stacy Patterson gripped the edge of her seat belt and watched the houses whiz by at sixty mph. *"Len, please, you have to slow down!"* she shouted desperately over the roar of the souped-up engine. "This is a school zone."

Behind the wheel of the lethal black Trans Am, her ex-husband seemed oblivious to all but the inner voices raging at him. Beneath the bill of the dark blue SWAT team cap he was no longer entitled to wear, his once-handsome face was grotesquely contorted. The mask of madness, one of his psychiatrists had termed it.

"I told you I'd find you, bitch, and I'm not letting you leave me again!" he shouted before baring his teeth in a manic smile. As if to emphasize his sick triumph, he deliberately accelerated, rocketing the sports coupe around a curve so fast the tires screeched. Flung hard against the belt, Stacy felt the rear of the Trans Am fishtailing violently and screamed a warning.

Len sliced **off** an obscenity and jerked the wheel. For an instant she thought he had regained control, only to catch sight of a towering pine tree looming directly ahead. Too terrified to scream, she curled forward against the belt's restraint in a desperate attempt to protect the fragile life in her belly.

The impact threw her violently forward against the dash before the belt drew her back. Like a hot poker, pain stabbed through her head. Her last thought before the blackness closed in was of the child she carried.

High on the scaffolding that encircled the three-story Victorian remodel's elaborate turret, Boyd MacAuley was methodically installing a new stained-glass window when he heard the earsplitting din of a violent collision. He knew even before he turned toward the sound that another unsuspecting driver had missed the notorious Astoria Street corkscrew turn and smashed headlong into the already scarred Douglas fir across the street.

With the sound of crunching metal still reverberating in his ears, he vaulted onto the ladder and headed down fast, leaping the last four feet to the ground just as the door to the small cottage next door slammed open.

"Call 911!" he shouted to the skinny nine-year-old girl who emerged. Without a word, Heidi Lanier made an abrupt about-face and disappeared inside.

As he sprinted across the grass toward the automobile, Boyd took quick stock of the situation. The vintage Trans Am that had collided with the massive fir was far too dated a model to have air bags. And if the occupants weren't wearing their belts... Hoping for the best, he prepared himself for the worst.

The car had hit head-on, and the front end had jammed into the massive trunk with such force it had compressed the hood like a flimsy soda can. On impact, the driver had obviously gone through the windshield and lay sprawled facedown amidst shattered glass on the slanted hood. Bigger than most men, the driver appeared to be in his mid-thirties and, from the angle of the neck, not destined to get any older.

Even before Boyd skidded to a stop next to the wreck, he was tugging off one grimy leather work glove. Gasping for air, yet forcing himself to remain calm, he touched two fingers to the man's carotid artery and prayed to feel even a faint pulse. Just as he'd suspected, the driver was dead or so close to it he doubted that even a fully equipped trauma team could save him.

Cursing the man's folly at not wearing his seat belt, Boyd peered through the shattered windshield at the female passenger who was slumped forward against the seat belt, masses of curly brown hair obscuring her facial features.

A small woman with slender shoulders, she was dressed in a sloppy man's shirt and shorts, and from what he could see, she appeared to be in her late twenties. There was a smear of blood on her head and blood on the dash, and she wasn't moving.

Damn, he thought as he hurried around the rear of the car and reached for the door handle on the passenger side. The shiny chrome was blistering hot against his palm, and the door refused to budge, no matter how hard he jerked. Either the blasted thing was locked or the car's frame had been sprung in the collision. He was about to make a dash for his truck and the pry bar in the rear tool compartment when he saw the woman in the passenger's seat stirring.

"Ma'am? Can you hear me?" he shouted through the glass. "Ma'am?"

Was someone calling her? Stacy turned her head and struggled to see through a haze of throbbing pain. It seemed an effort to blink, more of an effort to breathe. Ahead of her was a wall of greenery from the tree they'd hit.

Fighting off waves of sickness, she slowly swiveled her head back toward the driver's seat, then wished she hadn't. From a distance she heard buzzing in her head and felt her skin grow clammy. She'd fainted once during the early days of her pregnancy and recognized the warning signs.

"Ma'am? Listen to me."

The voice seemed to come from very far away. Stacy blinked, turned back toward the window. For a moment she'd forgotten the man on the other side of the glass. With great effort she managed to bring the man's form into sharper focus.

She saw his belt buckle first, cinching a low-slung carpenter's belt over worn and dirty jeans. Above stretched a corded male torso the color of old bronze, which glistened under a fine sheen of sweat. His chest was massive, its obvious strength scarcely softened by a triangle of damp blond chest hair. His brawny arms were corded from the effort he was making to tug open the car door. Numbly she realized that he was trying to help her.

"Please help my ex-husband!" she cried.

He glanced past her, his face tightening for an instant before he returned his gaze to her face. She saw the truth in his eyes and felt a sob rising from her chest, part rage, part grief.

"He's dead, isn't he?" Her voice was hollow, a mere whisper.

From the questioning look that flashed in his eyes, she realized he couldn't hear her through the glass. "Ma'am, can you unlock the door?"

Stacy blinked, tried to focus on her rescuer's face through the streaked window glass. Though his features were partially shadowed by the brim of a straw cowboy hat, she made out the bold slash of tawny brows over deep-set eyes the color of tempered steel and a not-quite straight nose. His mouth was wide and compressed into a hard line.

"Ma'am? The door?"

Summoning what remained of her wits, she forced herself to focus. "It's…not locked," she said through cold lips.

"Jammed," the man grated. At least that's what she managed to make out. The thudding in her head was making it difficult to concentrate. After staring down at her for a second, he straightened and pulled something from his belt. A hammer, she realized after a moment of fierce concentration.

"I'm going to have to break the glass. I need you to cover your face," he yelled.

Break the glass? That made sense, she thought and managed a nod before burying her face in hands that felt icy. She heard a crack, felt pebbles of safety glass showering her side, and cried out. A few seconds later, she lifted her head and saw him butting the remainder of the cracked glass from the window frame with huge, gloved hands. Then, with what looked like tremendous effort, he gripped the doorframe, braced his left foot on the side panel and pulled. Metal ground against metal in an earsplitting screech but refused to yield.

"Damn," he muttered, easing his grip long enough to wipe the sweat from his eyes with the back of one thick wrist. Teeth bared, tendons straining under bronzed skin, he tried again. Just when she was sure he would injure himself, the door yielded. An instant later she felt a blast of hot air hit her with the force of a freshly stoked furnace. She winced, blinked in the harsh glare, then tried to figure out what she was supposed to do next.

As though sensing her disorientation, her rescuer slowly squatted on his haunches, one tanned hand braced on the doorframe while he eased the seat belt from its latch with the other. He had removed his gloves, she noticed, and tucked them under his belt. He had large, rough hands, nicked here and there, and the wide, corded forearms of a working man.

She licked her lips and tried to formulate the words to thank him, only to have her train of thought interrupted by another voice close at hand. "Is she all right?"

Another face appeared in her field of vision. A young girl, waif thin, hovering at the stranger's side. She looked to be nine or ten at the most—and terrified. Stacy tried to reassure her but found she had no strength.

"She's going to be fine," the man answered before asking curtly, "Is the ambulance on the way?"

"Yes, the lady at 911 said five minutes—"

"Which means at least ten because of the sewer work on Fifteenth," he bit off impatiently.

"And she said to be sure and not move any of the passengers."

"Right." He leaned forward, his large body shielding Stacy from the searing sunshine. It hurt to draw the scorching air into her lungs, and yet she'd never felt so chilled. The shivers started inside, like a flood of icy water through her veins. When her teeth started to chatter, he uttered an oath before commanding, "Heidi, run and get a blanket from your house."

"Be right back," the girl told him before taking off running.

"I...shouldn't be...c-cold," Stacy breathed between shudders.

"Won't be long and you'll be tucked into a nice warm ambulance." He swept off his hat and dropped it to the ground outside the car. His hair was thick and blond and damp where wisps of lazy curls had been plastered to his forehead by the hatband.

"An h-hour ago I was w-wishing for w-winter."

His grin flashed, but his dark gray eyes remained probing as he pulled a folded handkerchief from his back pocket and gently blotted her temple. When the folded linen came away drenched in blood, she stared in bewilderment.

"Are you feeling any pain in your neck or your back?"

"No," she mumbled, then winced as another savage pain stabbed her temple. He swept his gaze lower, past her swollen breasts to the bulge beneath her oversize paint-spattered shirt.

"Damn, you're pregnant!" His tone was so harsh she blinked.

"Yes. Isn't it wonderful?"

His expression told her he didn't appreciate her joy. "How far along are you?"

She tried to smile the way she always did when she thought of the tiny little body that seemed to get bigger every day. "Just past seven months."

His jaw tightened, flexing muscle and sinew, and a look she could only describe as tortured traversed the hard planes.

"Who's your obstetrician?"

"I don't have one yet," she admitted, glancing away from his suddenly narrowed gaze. "I've only been in town a few weeks." After Len's depressingly frank doctors had begged her to leave, for her own safety.

"When was the last time you had an ultrasound?" he demanded an instant before the girl he'd called Heidi came running up with a multihued knitted afghan clutched to her thin chest. Stacy tried to smile her thanks, but her lips felt wooden.

"Oh God, there's a man...is he dead?" the girl cried in a frightened tone. Stacy saw the child's eyes glazing over and realized she'd just noticed Len's motionless body.

Her rescuer stood and turned, putting his wide chest between the child and her view of the hood. "Heidi, I need you to stay calm, for this lady's sake," he ordered in a gentle yet no-nonsense tone.

"I'll t-try." The girl sounded dazed, and Stacy's heart went out to her.

"I'm sorry," Stacy said softly.

"She can handle it, can't you, toots?" The big man wrapped the girl in his arms for a hard hug before holding her at arm's length. "Now, go call 911 again, and then stay in the house in case the operator calls back. Okay?"

"Okay."

Stacy watched the girl run across the street, her long blond hair flying. "Is she your daughter?" Her voice sounded strangely distant, as though she were speaking through layers of cotton.

"No, she's just a kid who comes home to an empty house. She's gotten into the habit of hanging around the job while I'm working." His face tightened for an instant before he bent forward to tuck the soft wool around Stacy's shivering body.

She saw then that his golden hair was lashed with strands of silver and smelled like sawdust, and his big bare shoulders were covered with a mixture of golden freckles and a fine layer of grit.

"Warmer now?"

Stacy tried to nod, but even that slight movement sent pain lancing through her skull. "Th-thanks," she said when the pain eased slightly.

"You say you just moved to town?"

"After my divorce was final." She started to turn her head toward the driver's side, but he placed a hand against her cheek, stopping her. "Len never accepted the d-divorce. His doctors thought it would be better to make a clean break."

She saw the questions in his eyes. And sympathy.

"Doctors?"

"He'd been in and out of...of a mental hospital in Washington for the past two years. I thought he was back in until he came to my apartment with a g-gun. Made me g-go with him."

Her rescuer bit off an expletive even as he darted a quick look at the driver's seat and floor. She saw the nine millimeter at the same time as he did, wedged between the clutch and brake, and shuddered. A siren wailed in the distance, growing louder quickly.

"About time," the man muttered, glaring toward the sound for a moment before turning his dark gray eyes on her face again. "It won't be long now. You'll be in good hands."

"You're very k-kind, Mr. uh…" She stopped, searching for a name, then realized he hadn't given her one.

"Boyd MacAuley."

"I'm…Stacy Patterson." She slipped a hand free of the blanket and held it out. His big hand closed over hers, his rough fingers wonderfully warm and reassuring. Woozy now, she let her eyes close. She would rest now, for just a moment, she told herself. Until the dizziness eased up.

"Hang on tight, Mrs. Patterson," she heard him say, and for the first time in months she felt safe.

Portland General Hospital was solid and square and resembled a brick fortress. Located in the downtown rabbit warren sandwiched between the Willamette River and the majestic Columbia, it had felt like home to Boyd the instant he'd first walked through the front door as a scared intern eight years ago. Now, however, it was just a place he didn't want to be.

As soon as the paramedic driving the ambulance had backed into the reserved space directly in front of the emergency room door, Boyd stepped from the back of the rig and squared his shoulders. Though Mrs. Patterson had fainted shortly before help had arrived and was still unconscious, her vitals were steady and she seemed in no great danger. Once she was safely in the hands of the trauma staff, his responsibility was ended.

Ten minutes tops, he told himself as he followed the two EMTs pushing the stretcher through the automatic sliding doors. Long enough for him to relate to the triage nurse all he'd learned before she'd passed out. Long enough to make sure she was getting the best Portland General had to offer.

Inside, there was an atmosphere of controlled urgency. Nurses in scrubs and doctors with surgical masks dangling under their chins moved swiftly yet with a sense of purpose that Boyd had once shared. Little had changed at PortGen in three years, he realized as he drew a deep breath of hospital air. It smelled the same, part dust and old wax, part disinfectant, and an unwanted rush of memories crashed over him.

He went cold inside and the floor seemed to shift. Fisting his hands at his sides, he drew in great gulps of air, fighting against the sharp claws of fury. Slowly the chill receded, bit by bit, until he could breathe normally again.

Around him, the controlled urgency took form and shape. And sound.

"Cubicle four, gentlemen," the admitting clerk barked as the paramedics slowed. Boyd didn't recognize the woman, but he knew the type—a drill sergeant with a clipboard and absolutely no sense of humor. More than once during his years as an intern and resident in this place, he'd tangled with this one's clone. The best he'd managed during all that time was a draw.

"Are you a relative, sir?" the clerk asked while strafing his naked chest with a disapproving gaze.

"No, just a witness." He saw the militant glint in her eyes and was about to brush past her when he heard a familiar voice calling his name. Turning toward the sound, he felt a jolt of relief. Prudence Randolph was the best nurse he'd encountered in the five years he'd spent practicing medicine. She was also his neighbor and his friend.

"So that really *is* the reclusive Boyd MacAuley under that gorgeous tan?" Prudy was an irrepressible tease and a charming flirt, but only with men she considered safe. She'd been divorced for years and claimed to have sworn off marriage forever.

"Sawdust is more like it," he replied, suddenly conscious of his sweat-stained jeans and grimy skin. No doubt he smelled like the mangy dog he resembled.

Prudy flicked him a curious grin, even as she was focusing her intelligent brown eyes on the patient. "Is she a friend of yours?"

"Never saw her before. Said her name's Stacy Patterson. We weren't able to find a purse or any identification."

"Auto accident?"

He raked a hand through his hair and nodded. "Trans Am hit a tree on Astoria. She was in the passenger's seat. From what I can tell she banged her head on impact." He drew a hard breath. "She's pregnant. Just over seven months. No attending OB."

Prudy's eyes clouded. "Vitals?" she asked the uniformed paramedic on the other side of the stretcher.

While the EMT recounted the numbers, Boyd searched the young woman's face for signs of returning consciousness. The gash on her forehead was oozing blood into the bandage applied by the paramedics, and her skin was purpling around the wound.

Small boned and too thin, she reminded him of a priceless porcelain doll his grandmother had kept on her dresser. Her skin had the same translucent quality as the fragile china, and her lashes were long and thick. Lost in the oblivion of sleep, she seemed very young and vulnerable—and terribly alone. It hurt to look at her, and yet he couldn't make himself walk away.

"Call Dr. Hoy," Prudy told the clerk briskly. "And get a lab tech up here stat. We'll need blood work done." The clerk flicked Boyd a curious glance before she turned to leave. He could almost predict the questions she would ask Prudy later.

"What about the driver?" Prudy asked as she held back the curtain to number four.

Boyd hesitated, the image of death still vivid in his mind. "The poor guy went through the windshield. Looked like a broken neck."

Prudy sighed. "Her husband?"

"Ex, I think she said."

"Is he the baby's father?"

Boyd raked back the still-damp hair that had flopped onto

his forehead. "She was pretty woozy and a little sparse on the details, but yeah, that seems a good bet."

Prudy frowned. "Ex or not, it's still going to be rough on her when she wakes up, especially if she loses the baby, too."

Yeah, it's always hardest on the one who's "lucky" enough to survive, Boyd thought as he watched Prudy and the two paramedics transfer Stacy to the narrow bed. There was a slash of yellow paint on one high cheekbone and yellow splatters on the bright pink basketball sneaker peeking out from the gray ambulance blanket tucked around her small form.

"Oops, sorry." Jenkins, the senior medic shot Boyd an apologetic glance, and Boyd realized that he was in the way. He'd forgotten for the moment that he was a carpenter now, a blue-collar guy with callused hands more suited to holding a hammer than a scalpel. Though his profession had changed, his knowledge of medicine hadn't, however. He waited until the paramedics left, then cleared his throat. "Who's the OB on call?"

"Jarrod." Prudy looked up from the blood pressure cuff she was affixing to the patient's too-thin arm and smiled. "We'll take good care of her, Boyd. The best. She'll be fine."

"Yeah, sure she will." A sudden lump pressed his throat and he had to swallow twice before he could make it dissolve. He'd heard that before. He'd even believed it. He knew better now. "Guess I'll head on back then."

Taking another step backward toward the curtain had him nearly colliding with an entering tech who sidestepped gingerly. "Sorry," Boyd muttered, and earned himself a pained look.

"Sir, you'll have to wait outside until after the doctor examines your wife," the tech instructed impatiently.

"She's not…" He stopped, realizing that the tech wasn't listening. Frowning, he turned to go, only to be halted by the sound of Mrs. Patterson's soft voice.

"No, wait. I don't…want him to go." Across the cubicle, Mrs. Patterson was now awake and watching him with bruised eyes. When he locked his gaze on hers, she tried to smile. "I haven't thanked you."

He cleared his throat. "No need. Mostly I just kept you company until the bus showed up."

Stacy wet her lips and struggled to focus her mind on her rescuer's words instead of the all-encompassing pain in her head. "Bus?"

"Sorry, I mean the ambulance." His mouth quirked. It wasn't quite a smile but held a certain promise she found endearing.

"I don't...but of course, there would have to be...an ambulance. How silly of me...not to remember."

The effort to speak set her head to spinning, and she hauled in air in an effort to clear her brain. Concentrate on his eyes, she told herself as his face wavered in and out of focus. Gray eyes in a deeply tanned face. Quicksilver eyes, framed by thick, blunt lashes the color of bronze. There was something haunting about those eyes. Something sad. Memories he didn't want, perhaps, or lingering shadows of a terrible suffering. For an instant, she thought she was looking into the eyes of her tormented husband.

"Boyd?" she murmured, and heard his deep voice answering. The words were indistinct, yet she felt a sense of comfort.

Another face swam into her field of vision. A face with feminine features and a kind smile. A face topped by a halo of shining copper. A nurse, she finally decided.

"Is there anyone you want us to call for you, Mrs. Patterson? Family? Friends?"

Stacy concentrated for a moment. "Some...someone should call my ex-in-laws in Seattle. Leonard Patterson, Sr., on Stanton Street." Old and frail now, the Pattersons had never forgiven her for signing the papers to commit their only son.

Someone repeated the information, then asked if there was anyone else. A member of her own family perhaps? The baby's father?

"Len..."

"Len was the baby's father?" the voice repeated with a soothing calm.

"Yes." Len had longed to become a father, but that was before a hopped-up kid bent on robbery had split his skull with a baseball bat. After that, he'd become a mean, angry man given to bouts of violence that had finally worn out her love and her loyalty.

"Anyone else? A neighbor, maybe? Or a co-worker?"

Stacy cleared her throat again of a sudden thickness and searched for the name that hovered just beyond her consciousness. A face wavered, round and patrician, with a frizz of curly white hair swooping over the apple cheeks. "Adeline... Marsh."

"Is she a friend?"

"Principal at Lewis and Clark Elementary. I've been substituting. Morning kindergarten." Stacy licked her lips, aware suddenly that somehow, her hand was in Boyd's again. Had she reached for him? Or had he reached for her? Either way, she was grateful for the human contact and curled her fingers tighter around his.

"I'm...sorry about taking you away from your work," she murmured, her voice oddly thin.

"It'll still be there when I get back." He bent lower, and his bare shoulders blocked out the overhead light.

"Will your boss be angry?"

"No boss. I work alone."

She heard a low drone of whispered conversation and turned her head toward the sound. The resulting pain in her temple caused her to inhale sharply.

"Easy, honey," he soothed, his voice low and scratchy.

Slowly she adjusted the angle of her head until she could see his eyes, now dark and intense and probing. Deep lines fanned the outer corners, suggesting a man who knew how to laugh, yet the strongly molded face had the look of a man more accustomed to discipline and control and restraint.

"Miz Patterson?" a third voice inquired softly. "I need to draw blood for the lab now."

It wasn't really a question, saving Stacy the trouble of replying. Boyd stepped back to allow room for a roly-poly woman in a blue smock. Stacy watched anxiously as the woman readied a syringe and hoped she wouldn't disgrace herself by fainting. Just in case, she looked away before the needle entered her arm.

She felt a prick, then pressure. The overhead light was beginning to sear her eyes, and her head was spinning again. She felt her lashes drooping and quickly forced her eyes wider. It was important to stay awake and alert. In control.

"Boyd?" Mindless of her aching head, she looked around anxiously.

"Right here, Stacy." He took her hand again, and the cold that had begun to seep into her again abated. The self-confidence she'd built up over the past year was crumbling fast, leaving her feeling lost and scared and lonely.

Some independent woman you are, she thought, disgusted with her pitiful lack of fortitude. Here she was, an expectant mother who wanted desperately to be held in the arms of a man she'd just met.

She started to thank him again, only to find herself seized by a spasm of pain in the small of her back. She stopped breathing, her heart tripping. The pain spread, rippling toward her belly, nearly squeezing her in two.

"No!" she cried in sharp agony. "It's too soon!"

"Get Dr. Jarrod, stat," she heard the nurse order sharply. "Tell him the patient may be going into premature labor."

Stacy clung to the strong hand wrapping hers, terror racing with the adrenaline in her veins.

"Try to relax, Stacy. Take deep breaths." Boyd's voice was steady and calm, everything she wasn't.

"Tell them to save the baby," she pleaded. "Make them promise. If there's a choice, my baby has to live."

"Look, babies are surprisingly resilient, especially in utero," he said in that curiously raspy voice.

"But what if she isn't? What if—"

"Hey, none of that, okay?" Lifting a hand from hers, he brushed back a lock of her hair, his touch as gentle as a lover's caress. "You're going to be fine. Both of you."

Stacy tightened her grip on his hand. "Is that a p-promise, or a guess?"

His hesitation was slight but noticeable. Because he didn't want to lie? she wondered.

"Definitely a promise," he declared an instant before the curtains parted to admit a tall, lanky man who, in spite of the blue scrubs, reminded her more of a working cowboy than a doctor.

"MacAuley?" he exclaimed on a double take. "What the hell?"

"Later," Boyd said, stepping back. He'd done all he could do for the dark-haired angel with the beautiful eyes. Now it was up to the professionals. And luck. It had been a long time since he'd allowed himself to believe in either one.

# Two

Boyd thumbed open his third can of beer, drank deeply, then wandered out of the kitchen onto the back porch. It was nearly seven, and the sun was hovering at the edge of the western horizon, turning the sky to flame, while the conifers that typified the Oregon skyline suggested black teeth eating the sunset inch by inch. Below the ridge that wedged downward at a sharp angle, the Columbia River resembled molten lava as the sun's rays skimmed the surface.

Propping a bare foot on the railing, he leaned forward slightly, hoping to catch a breeze, but the air was deathly still. At the house to the left, Linda and Marshall Ladd were barbecuing burgers. At the end of the short street, Portland firefighter, Cliff Balisky, was roughhousing with his two boys, who from the sound of their triumphant shouts were whomping up on the old man.

Suddenly restless, he chugged down the rest of the beer in his hand and gave some thought to opening another. How long had it been since he'd been drunk enough to pass out? Drunk enough to buy himself a few hours of mindless oblivion? Four, five months maybe? Longer?

Before Karen and the baby had died, he'd never been much of a drinker, mostly because he didn't like the reckless edge it put on his personality. Tonight, however, the need for numbness had overridden his customary caution.

He knew the reason for his black mood. The ambulance ride, the all-too-familiar bustle of the ER. A baby in danger. A wisp of a woman with big green eyes and a tumble of silk-soft hair who'd somehow slipped beneath his guard and touched a part of him he'd thought he'd lost.

The woman was fine, he assured himself firmly as he headed inside for another beer. Definitely in good hands and no doubt still sleeping peacefully, just as she'd been when he'd left her a couple of hours ago. Still, his conscience would likely give him fits unless he made sure, he decided as he reached for the wall phone by the kitchen window.

Though the hospital switchboard was known for its efficiency, it took the operator an interminable five minutes to track down Prudy, another minute before he heard her calm voice in his ear.

"I thought you might be calling," she said after he'd identified himself.

"The hell you did." Boyd glowered at his reflection in the window over the sink. He was already regretting the impulse to call.

"In answer to your question—"

"What question? All I did was say hello."

"She's resting comfortably."

Boyd heard the teasing note in Prudy's tired voice and felt his patience thinning. "Are you going to tell me what I want to know or am I going to be banging on your door at five a.m. for the next week?"

Prudy groaned. "You sure know how to bargain from strength, you rat."

"A man's got to do—"

"Okay, okay." He heard laughter in her tone and felt the tension clawing his spine ease off a notch. "She's concussed, which you already know, has a severe sprain of the left ankle and an impressive collection of bruises.''

Boyd cleared his throat and squared his shoulders. ''And the baby?''

''So far so good, although **Mrs.** Patterson's been spotting. Jarrod has her on a fetal monitor and an IV drip, mag sulfate. The fetal heartbeat is strong and steady.''

Boyd acknowledged that with a grunt. It was exactly what he would have done. ''What's Jarrod's prognosis?''

''Guardedly optimistic.''

He lifted a hand to the back of his neck and methodically kneaded the tension-twisted muscles. ''Do me a favor and read me Jarrod's notes, okay?''

''You know I can't do that,'' Prudy exclaimed softly through the wire.

''Why the hell not?''

''Come on, Boyd. You know the rules about a patient's right to privacy as well as I do. You're not a relative and you're not on staff, so therefore—''

''Screw the rules. Tell me.''

''No.''

He felt his face growing hot. ''Since when did you become so righteous, Ms. Holier-Than-Thou?'' As soon as the words left his mouth he wanted to call them back.

The silence at the other end was more damning than a curse, and he drew a long breath in an attempt to level the sudden spike of anger that had had him speaking before he thought. Prudy was the last person he wanted to hurt. As friends go, she was the best. After the accident, she'd taken care of him like a persistent little mother hen, there for him when he'd needed someone. He'd been close to losing it then, closer than he wanted to recall. He'd battled back to a semblance of normality by burying his memories along with his ability to care too deeply for anything or anyone.

''I'm sorry, that was out of line,'' he said when the silence grew longer than he could handle.

''She really got to you, didn't she?'' Prudy questioned quietly.

"Yeah, I guess she did." More than he wanted to accept.
"Boyd—"

He heard the sympathy in Prudy's voice and ruthlessly cut
her off. He could handle the past as long as it remained buried.
"Give her my best, okay?" He hung up before Prudy could
say more.

Stacy woke to the echo of a scream. Her own, she realized
with a pounding heart and drenched skin. She felt queasy and
heavy, and her ankle throbbed. Disoriented, she turned toward
a glimmer of light to her left, then wished she hadn't as the
dull pain in her head took on star-burst edges.

The room's bare white walls were shadowed. The narrow
bed came equipped with side rails and was slab hard. The
pillow beneath her aching head was only marginally softer.
Still, she was thankful that she and the baby were alive and
in good hands.

In the hospital, she recalled with relief. And for the moment,
safe. The image of Len sprawled on the hood flashed into her
mind again, and she shuddered. The baby was what mattered,
all that mattered.

*Babies are surprisingly resilient, especially in utero.*

She drew a breath, thinking about the man who'd spoken
those words earlier. Sweet, calming, positive words from a
man with sawdust in his hair and calluses on his hands. A man
accustomed to taking charge, she realized now. A quiet sort
of guy with smoky eyes and a raspy voice. A powerful male
with raw edges, a hard, arrogant mouth with surprisingly sensitive corners, and a don't-tread-on-me air riding those burly
carpenter's shoulders. There wasn't a reason in the world why
she should feel as though she'd known him—and trusted
him—for a very long time, but she did.

Sleepy now, she let her mind linger on the image of an off-
center smile and kind eyes in a deeply tanned face. Fathom-
less, intelligent eyes with whispers of pain still lingering in
devil-dark pupils, framed by laugh lines suggesting a sense of
humor.

His mouth, too, had given a hint of that same humor, a faint upward tilt at the corners of those aggressively masculine lips. More pronounced was the threat of an intensely male sensuality, the kind that had her fantasizing about lazy rain-washed afternoons spent in a man's arms in front of a warming, pine-scented fire. And when he'd smiled—once—she'd felt oddly cherished, as though he'd brushed those hard lips over hers.

Drowsy now, she brought her fingers to her lips and felt them curve into a languid smile. Ships in the night, she thought. Destined for different ports. She doubted she would see him again, but for the rest of her life she would always have a special place in her heart for a very special, rough, tough-as-nails Good Samaritan. She was still thinking about him when she drifted off.

"Oatmeal is *wonderful*. I truly, absolutely *love* oatmeal. Oatmeal is my friend."

Stacy sighed and looped another circle in the lumpy stuff beneath her spoon. She was hungry, the baby was awake and hammering on her insides with tiny fists as though she, too, were eager for breakfast, and yet, Stacy couldn't seem to work up the courage to swallow that first mouthful.

"It's just that it tastes like used wallpaper paste," she muttered to the empty glass that had held eight ounces of milk only a few minutes earlier. That, at least, she'd learned to stomach during the first few weeks after she'd found out about the baby. But oatmeal?

"Definitely a challenge."

Using her free hand, she raised the head of the bed a few inches more by pressing the button on the railing, then ran her tongue over her lips. Okay, this is for the baby, she thought as she grimly scooped up a tiny spoonful. She had it halfway to her mouth before she realized she had an audience.

Her Good Samaritan was standing just inside the door, a ragged bouquet of pink blossoms in his hands and a crooked smile on his deeply tanned face. Gone was the day's growth of beard that had given his face an outlaw appeal. His hair, now shiny clean and neatly brushed, was an intriguing mix of gold and platinum and silver blended into a unique color she could only call dusty blond.

Unlike yesterday, he was fully clothed in a chest-hugging T-shirt of faded blue, sporting the logo of a local lumberyard, and tight jeans worn thin from the stress of hard muscle rubbing against unyielding seams.

"This is just a guess, but I have a hunch you're not crazy about PortGen's breakfast special," he said, widening his smile into a truly dazzling but all-too-brief grin bracketed by engaging creases.

When she realized she was drinking in the sight of him like a parched desert nomad in sight of a spring, she quickly lowered her gaze to the spoon and shuddered. "I can't believe there are actually people who order this stuff on purpose."

She heard him chuckle and glanced his way again. Their gazes met, and she found herself holding her breath. More alert now, she decided that his irises weren't merely gray, but intensely so, the color of sooty topaz shot through with silver.

It had been forever since she'd felt such an instant attraction to a man, and she'd learned since not to trust any feeling that flashed so hot and fast. Still, she couldn't prevent her heart from skipping and her lips from curving as she feigned indignation.

"I'm starving to death, and the man is laughing," she groused to the ceiling.

"Sorry," he said, coming closer, adding the fresh tang of soap to the hospital mix. "I forgot myself for a moment."

Stacy felt her spirits reviving. After months of unremitting tension and fear, it felt good to smile again, even if it did hurt to move her facial muscles. "I'll forgive you, but only because you saved my life yesterday."

"Nah, wearing your seat belt saved your life."

She didn't waste breath arguing with a man whose jaw had taken on the texture of mountain granite. Instead, she directed an inquiring look at the fluffy blooms held in an awkward, one-handed grip against his flat belly.

"The hydrangeas are beautiful."

His eyebrows drew together and she noticed a faint scar

angling across the left one in a jagged line. "Is that what they are?"

She nodded, then realized she was still holding the spoon and carefully returned it to the breakfast tray before pushing the table toward the foot of the bed. "I feel better just looking at them."

She smiled, drawing Boyd's gaze for an instant to her lips. Most guys he knew were suckers for the kind of impudent dimples framing her mouth. Thank the saints he was immune, he thought a smug instant before he found himself wondering if her pale, full lips would taste sweet. Like the wild berries that soaked up sugar-producing summer sunshine along the country roads.

When he felt heat climbing his neck, he frowned down at the sissy-looking flowers. He'd bought flowers for a patient before, but he'd always had the florist downstairs deliver them, and without a card.

"Maybe the nurse has a vase," she said, reaching for the call button.

"No need. This'll do fine," He stuffed the flowers into her water jug before she could argue the point. Then feeling awkward and more than a little foolish, he shoved his hands into his hip pockets and took a step backward. It was time he returned to work.

"I'm glad you came by," she said before he had a chance to get the hell out of there. "I wanted to ask you about that little girl who was so helpful and sweet. Um, Heidi, wasn't it?"

He nodded. "What can I tell you? She's a lonely little kid with too much imagination and not enough of the good stuff parents are supposed to provide."

"I'd like to do something to express my appreciation to her as soon as...as..." She halted and drew a breath that seemed to drain more than invigorate. "What would she like, do you think?"

One of Stacy Patterson's smiles for starters, he thought, and then frowned. Where the hell did that come from?

"Hell if I know," he hedged.

"I was thinking of a CD, but I have no idea what kind of music she prefers."

"She hates country, I know that."

"Why?"

"Because she's always making remarks about my lousy taste in radio stations."

Her lips curved, and for an instant her eyes sparkled. He felt something loosen inside, and frowned. "I take it you listen to country," she asked, touching one of the blossoms with a caressing fingertip.

"When I'm working, yeah." He'd been thinking her eyes were green, but now he saw a hint of gold mingling in the depths. Sunshine pretty, he thought, and as warming as summer's rays.

He wanted to gather her close and bask in the warmth of that sweet, soft smile until he couldn't remember what it felt like to be a man on the outside of happiness, looking in, longing to feel strong and protective and loved by a woman he adored. But those days were gone. Lost.

"Uh, maybe I could find out for you," he said lamely. "The kind of music she likes."

"That would be great, thanks."

"No sweat." He pulled his hands from his pocket and glanced at his watch. "I'd best be heading out," he said, shifting. "I promised I'd have this job done in time for the owners' tenth anniversary, and time's getting short."

Was that disappointment he saw wisping across her gaze? Or relief to be rid of the blundering brute? He'd never been all that great at entertaining women. When he'd been a gawky kid working a couple of part-time jobs in order to save for college, he'd been too busy to learn the moves other guys had mastered by the time pimples gave way to whiskers.

In college, the women he'd met seemed all too willing to entertain *him*—once they found out he was headed for medical school and the big-bucks future. Now that he had an ordinary job with ordinary pay—well hell, he'd been boring even when he'd been a doctor. Even Karen had said as much more than once, but she'd put up with him for reasons he never fully understood.

After her death, he hadn't cared much one way or another about his skill with the ladies. But now he wished he could crack jokes like his kid brother, Ben, or flirt without coming on too strong or too awkward like his friend, Luke Jarrod—anything to arouse another sparkling smile in those now-somber emerald eyes.

"Thanks again," she murmured. "For the flowers." Before she shifted her gaze to the puffy bouquet he thought he saw moisture pooling in her eyes.

"I'm sorry about your ex-husband."

"So am I."

"He was in the hospital, you said?"

"He was hurt doing what he loved—protecting others." Stacy drew a suddenly shaky breath. "There were two of them robbing a convenience store near our house. They'd nearly beaten the clerk to death by the time Len had walked in to buy cigarettes. He'd drawn his gun, but the boys were so young—scarcely fourteen."

Boyd bit off a curse that had her pale lips trembling into a rueful smile that she couldn't sustain. "No one's really sure exactly how it happened. It doesn't really matter. What matters is that one of the boys hit Len in the head with a baseball bat he must have found behind the counter." She stopped to clear her throat. "By the time I got to the hospital, Len was in surgery. When he woke up, he was...changed."

"Brain damage?"

She nodded. "All cops have a capacity for violence or they wouldn't be cops. The good ones have a...an instinct for right and wrong that keeps that violence inside unless it's needed to protect human life. After his injury, Len had these rages that just...took over. And when that happened, he enjoyed hurting people."

"He hurt you?" His voice was too harsh, but there was nothing he could do about it, just as there was nothing he could do about the anger pouring through him at the thought of those huge wrestler's hands bruising her smooth skin.

"Not at first. He was more like a lost child. But...later, after he'd recovered physically, he had episodes."

She thought about the wild look of fear that had sometimes surfaced in his eyes when he'd thought he was being stalked by some nameless, faceless enemy. Some nights he'd sat up, waiting, his weapon cradled lovingly in his hands. Watching and waiting. She sighed, looked down at her hands.

"I had him committed twice. Once, after he stopped taking his medication and started drinking, and again, about six months later when he started showing up at the school where I was teaching." She drew in a lungful of air and held it for a long moment before releasing it slowly. "Several times he even got violent when there were children present, waiting for their bus. When I threatened to call the police, he cried and promised to stop. He seemed like his own self for a while and I started to think he was recovering. But when I found out I was pregnant, he got it into his head that the baby wasn't his and—" She couldn't go on. The memories were too vivid, too painful.

"I'm sorry, Stacy."

"It wasn't his fault. I know that." She forced a smile. "Len always wanted a daughter."

Boyd felt a hole open inside, a hole he'd thought he'd cemented tight. Suddenly the room seemed too small and the air too thin. Dumb move, coming back here, he thought, drawing in a long breath. "Guess I'll leave you to your breakfast," he said in a decent enough tone.

"I thought you were my friend," she muttered, glancing pointedly at her congealing breakfast.

He turned the idea of being her friend over in his mind and found he liked the idea more than he should. "Uh, I just came by to see how you're doing. Both of you."

"We're both feeling much better this morning. Dr. Jarrod removed the monitor this morning, and Tory is back to her usual rowdy antics. I expect her to become a world-class gymnast someday."

"Tory?"

"Mmm. Short for Victoria."

One side of his mouth quirked. "Nice name. Classy."

"You don't think it's a bit stuffy for this day and age?"
She inhaled, then rushed on. "I mean, the books all stress how
important a name can be in the development of a child's personality."

"No, it's not stuffy at all."

Stacy heard the sudden hoarseness in his voice, saw the
shutters come crashing down in his eyes. As though he were
retreating from the friendship she was offering—and her. So
she found herself utterly dumbfounded when he suddenly
reached out a hand to caress her bruised cheek. The gesture
was so utterly tender, the moment so intensely intimate she
forgot to breathe.

"I'm glad you're okay."

She swallowed the hard lump in her throat. "Believe me,
so am I."

"If there's anything I can do, anything you need—"

"No, but thank you," she assured him.

"Take care of yourself and Victoria," he said brusquely
before turning away. Two steps later he stopped and stood
motionless, staring at the stark white linoleum under his boots
as though searching for an answer to some deeply disturbing
question.

Stacy was about to ask him if she could help when he turned
and retraced his steps. Leaning forward, he braced one hand
flat on the mattress while the other gently cupped her shoulder.

"For luck," he murmured before he brought his mouth to
hers. Sweetly, with no demand, he kissed her, his lips soft and
searching, his breath scented with strong coffee and tooth-
paste.

A heartbeat later, he was gone, swallowed by the cavernous
hospital corridor, leaving her stunned and bemused. It was
only when she felt the tears dripping onto her breast that she
realized she was crying.

# Three

Stacy was still groggy from an afternoon nap when a strangely familiar, copper-haired nurse stuck her head in the door. A small woman, in a fuchsia-and-pink smock over pink slacks and yellow canvas sneakers, she reminded Stacy of a bright winter sunset.

"Hi, I'm Prudy Randolph. We met in the ER yesterday," she said when she saw that Stacy was awake.

"We did indeed," Stacy replied, waving her in. "I was hoping to get a chance to thank you for all your help."

Nurse Randolph shrugged off her thanks with an infectious grin that had Stacy's spirits lifting. "How're you feeling?"

"Antsy. I hate hospitals."

"On days like this, so do I."

Stacy laughed and found it felt good. "Feel free to hide out here with me. I promise I won't tattle."

"Sounds like an offer I can't refuse." Looking very much like a mischievous six-year-old playing a prank on her teacher, the elfin nurse pulled up the only chair and sat. "Lord, I'm bushed," she said, and let out with a heartfelt sigh. "And it's not even a full moon."

"Sounds like you've been inundated with accident victims."

"You have no idea." Prudy blew a lock of hair from her forehead before grimacing. "Everything from the usual fender-benders to a parrot attack."

Stacy blinked. "Parrot attack?"

"Hmm. On the owner. A case of adolescent rebellion mixed with rampaging hormones."

"The owner was a teenager?"

Prudy laughed. "No, the parrot. A male, naturally, and not at all happy to be kept away from the newest addition to the family bird population, which just happened to be a very attractive—and willing—female."

"Naturally."

Prudy swiped a hand through her Orphan Annie curls. "Sorry to unload on you. Sometimes I wish I'd followed my mother's advice and become a supermarket checker."

"At least the hours are better."

"Not to mention the pay."

Stacy laughed, then moaned at the sudden explosion of glittery light behind her eyes. Nurse Randolph's expression became solicitous. "Head still hurting?"

"Let's just say I've got a long way to go before I'm up to the 'feeling lousy' stage."

Chocolate brown eyes studied hers with professional expertise. "Any idea when Dr. Jarrod plans to release you?"

"This morning he said three or four days—*if* I continued to improve, and *if* there are no more indications of labor." She sighed. "Keep your fingers crossed for me."

Prudy pretended to take offense. "Hey, you sound as though you don't like our deluxe accommodations."

"I can't afford deluxe, or even economy class. I'm not even sure I can afford the cost of that box of tissues."

The nurse looked startled and then embarrassed. "If there's a problem, I could contact Social Services for you."

Stacy felt a sudden heat scalding her cheeks. The thought

of having to apply for public assistance made her uncomfortable. "Don't mind me," she said with a laugh to show she wasn't really concerned. "I'm addicted to worrying. It's my drug of choice."

"Sounds like my mother," Prudy said with a wry grimace. Settling back, she propped her feet against the bottom railing of the bed and yawned. "Sorry, it's the rotating shifts, not the company."

An ambulance was approaching below, its siren's wail growing steadily louder. Down the hall, a baby cried and a woman crooned. According to the aid who'd served her breakfast, the birthing rooms were full. Five rooms, five moms in labor.

"Nice flowers," Prudy said with a nod toward the hydrangeas. "I've got some just like that in my yard." Her eyes narrowed, then turned quizzical. "At least I did when I left this morning."

Stacy adjusted the head of the bed and tried to ignore the sudden craving for a pastrami sandwich and a kosher pickle. "My Good Samaritan brought them by earlier. You remember him? The man who came with me in the ambulance."

Prudy stretched out her legs and frowned. "Oh yeah, I remember him, all right. Boyd MacAuley, the flower-poaching rat."

Stacy frowned. "You know him?"

"He's my neighbor, and I'm going to kill him for stealing my pampered darlings, that's what I'm going to do." She sighed, then offered Stacy a look. "Not that I wouldn't have given him permission to pick them, mind you, but it would have been nice if he'd asked. Fat chance, though, since Boyd was never one for polite niceties."

Stacy fought a fast battle with herself—and lost. Curiosity might kill a cat, but she'd always considered herself more bulldog than feline. Besides, she had to know. "I...suppose he doesn't live alone."

"No, he lives with a ghost."

Stacy blinked. "Pardon?"

Prudy sat up and arched her back, as though working out a

few kinks. "Boyd's a widower. For more than three years now, but to all intents and purposes, Karen's still in that house."

"Karen is—was his wife?"

The nurse nodded. "She was a Waverly. Her family owns mills. The complex where Boyd and I live used to belong to her grandfather—along with half of Portland."

"What happened to her?"

"An auto accident, what else?" Prudy shook her head, her brown eyes sad. "Karen was seven months pregnant. Luke Jarrod tried to save the baby, a beautiful little girl who looked exactly like her daddy, but the poor little angel only lived a few minutes longer than her mother. After that, Boyd just shut down emotionally. For a long time I thought we might lose him, too."

Stacy thought back to the conversation she and Boyd had shared that morning—and the change that had come over him when she'd started gushing about the baby. No wonder he'd turned to stone.

A wave of embarrassment ran through her, followed closely by empathy for a man who'd lost so much and yet had been so quick to comfort a stranger.

"He's a nice man," she murmured, her voice thick.

"You like him, don't you?" Stacy heard sympathy in the other woman's voice and looked up slowly.

"Very much," she admitted, because there didn't seem to be a point in denying it. "I think I would have liked him even if he hadn't come racing to my rescue."

"Stacy—"

"Don't worry, I'm not mooning over the man," she assured the other woman whose clouded eyes and worried expression seemed to signal genuine concern. "Whatever romantic illusions I might have had about white knights and happily-ever-after endings faded a long time ago."

"Ain't that the truth?" A piercing sadness came and went in the other woman's eyes an instant before she curved her lips into a smile and stood up.

"Much as I hate to, I'd better get back down to the zoo. By this time the animals should be good and restless."

Ever conscious of the tenderness lurking in her skull, Stacy offered a restrained laugh and a look of commiseration that Prudy returned before slapping her palm gently against her forehead.

"For Pete's sake, I almost forgot the reason I came up in the first place," she muttered, shaking her head. "Yesterday, when I called the principal at the school where you're subbing, she said to give you her best regards and to tell you not to be in a stew about getting straight back to work. Something about a permanent position she thought might be opening up next September? I guess it fell through, so you're off the hook. I thought you'd like to know. There's nothing worse than being strapped to a bed when you think your world may be falling apart because you're on hiatus."

Off the hook? More like, out in the streets, Stacy thought. She gulped down a wave of disappointment and wondered why she always felt like laughing when disaster struck. Hysteria, no doubt. To say the least, it was not good news that the permanent position at the school had not come through.

"When it rains, it pours," she muttered, feeling suddenly battered on the inside, too.

"Bad news?" the coppery-haired nurse asked. "Geez, I'm sorry. I thought—" She waved a hand. "Well, it's obvious what I thought. Getting back to work is usually a major concern. I kind of hoped the news would ease your mind." She shot a disgruntled glance at the ceiling. "Good going, Prudy, old girl. Traumatize the patient with bulletins of disaster." She brought her gaze back down to Stacy. "Jarrod will have my hide."

Stacy couldn't help but chuckle, even though the gesture sent a pain lancing through her skull. "Hey, don't worry about it. Under normal circumstances, it would have eased my mind knowing I wasn't needed desperately at my workplace."

"Only your circumstances aren't normal?"

"And whose are?" Stacy asked with a tone of levity she

was far from feeling. "We women are the stronger gender, remember. I'll survive."

The question, at the moment, was how, she thought after she exchanged goodbyes with Prudy and watched her walk from the room. She'd been desperately hoping for the regular paycheck offered by a permanent position—and medical insurance for both her and the baby. At the moment she had neither. Every moment she spent in this hospital bed was costing her a fortune she didn't have, didn't even hope to have.

Wearily she closed her eyes, but the desperate worry that had been her constant companion for six long months was still there, hovering, reminding her that she had another life to consider, another soul to nurture.

Gently she pressed her hand against her womb and tried to imagine the face of the baby inside. Len had been an extremely striking man, with jet-black hair and startling blue eyes. Her own eyes were mostly hazel, unless she happened to be wearing green, and then they darkened to the color of moss.

All her life people had been marveling at her eyes and the thick dark lashes framing them. Her best feature, they'd invariably declared, the only physical attribute of hers she cared to pass along to her daughter. The rest of her was little better than average, except her height, which was a good three inches below the national mean of five-six.

No, Victoria would be tall and slender, with the grace of a ballerina, not saddled with her mother's two left feet and pear-shaped figure. Not if there was a God in heaven.

The smile that always formed when Stacy thought of her daughter faded, replaced by a frown that tugged painfully at the bruised parts of her face. She had exactly $226 in her checking account, a tiny studio apartment that was paid for through the end of the month only and one suitcase of clothes for both herself and the baby. Everything else had been left in the house in Wenatchee Falls. It was all gone now, burned up in the fire that Len had started in a rage over the separation.

Oh Tory, what are we going to do? she cried silently, feathering her fingers over the soft bulge where the baby lay. Even if she healed fast, it would be at least a week before she was presentable enough to enter a classroom without frightening the children half to death. Worse, the school year would soon be ending, leaving her without even the meager earnings she'd been earning as a sub.

Did McDonald's hire expectant moms? she wondered. Did anyone?

The thought of having to swallow her pride and apply for welfare was disturbing. But what else could she do if she couldn't find work? She was an only child. Her parents were both dead, and Len's parents had written her off.

She felt tears collecting in her eyes and blinked them away. What she needed now was a plan of action, a strategy to see her through the next three months until the baby was born and for at least six weeks after that. But what?

Think, Stace, she urged silently. Use that brilliant intellect you're supposed to have to come up with something...brilliant. Okay, forget brilliant, she amended after a moment's consideration. Just come up with something that will work.

Ten minutes later she was still trying when she heard a rap on the door. Wearily she opened her eyes to find a uniformed policeman standing in the doorway, looking ill at ease. For a frozen moment she thought it was Len standing there, returned from the dead to mock her.

"Mrs. Patterson? I'm Officer Klein from Portland P.D. traffic investigations. Do you feel up to giving me a statement about the accident yesterday?"

Shaking in relief, she cleared her throat and tried to marshal her thoughts. "There's not much to tell, Officer. My ex-husband was driving too fast and the car went out of control. We hit a tree and...and Len was killed. Leonard Patterson. He was a retired policeman, from the Wenatchee Falls, Washington, P.D."

The officer approached slowly, his gaze giving the room and her an instinctive inspection. "Yes, ma'am. I got an ID from the DMV and a description of the accident from the witness, Dr. MacAuley, but—"

"Oh no, Officer, Mr. MacAuley's a carpenter, not a doctor." Once again, she saw the hard, lean contours of Boyd's massive chest as he'd leaned over her. Muscles like those had been built up over a long stretch of hours spent in punishing physical labor.

"If you say so, ma'am, only the ID he showed me said he was an M.D."

Stacy furrowed her brow and thought about the steady note of confidence in his voice and the words he'd used. *In utero,* he'd said. At the time she hadn't noted the incongruity of the clinical usage and the sawdust frosting his massive shoulders.

"Perhaps I was mistaken," she murmured.

The officer shifted his feet and glanced down at the yellow sheet of paper in his hand. "Ma'am, according to the registration we found in the glove box, the Trans Am is in your name as well as your ex-husband's. Is that correct?"

"I don't know. To tell you the truth I just assumed that Len had changed that when the divorce was final."

Officer Klein nodded before consulting his notes once more. "There are charges for towing," he said when he glanced up again. "Since the insurance has lapsed, the owner is liable."

Stacy stared, her mouth open, her breath stilled, unwilling to take in the words. When the officer began to look acutely uncomfortable, she realized that she was expected to respond. "How...much for towing?" she said.

"One hundred and seventy-five dollars." This time there was no mistaking the apology in his tone. Lord, she must really look pathetic, she thought as she nodded slowly. Two hundred and twenty-six minus one-hundred and seventy-five was...fifty-one? Surely that couldn't be right, she thought desperately. But it was.

"Leave the bill and I'll send you a check as soon as I get back to my apartment."

"Yes, ma'am." But instead of handing her the bill, the man continued to stand stiffly, his expression troubled.

"Is there something else?" she demanded, resigned to taking the bad news stoically, like nasty medicine.

The officer glanced around, as though looking for backup,

and Stacy's heart rate accelerated. "It's okay, Officer. I promise I won't go for your throat."

That won her a brief smile and an appreciative salute from those cautious blue eyes. "Uh, there's also a storage fee."

"How much?"

"Twenty-five dollars a day."

Stacy couldn't decide whether to laugh or cry. She figured the baby would appreciate laughter more than tears, but even as she curved her lips into a smile, she felt the hot press of tears in her throat.

"Leave that bill, too," she said in a voice that wasn't quite steady.

"Yes, ma'am."

"And then do me a favor, okay? Blow the darn wreck to kingdom come."

The young officer dropped the paper onto the bed tray next to the bright, lacy bouquet and fled. It was a long time before Stacy could stop shaking.

# Four

"**P**lease, please answer," Stacy pleaded silently, but the phone on the other end continued to ring and ring. When the receiver began to feel welded to her ear, she reluctantly gave up and let the receiver drop into the cradle on the table by the bed.

"Nobody home?"

The voice was sand over steel and familiar. Her heart was speeding even before she turned her gaze toward the man who'd uttered the words.

Boyd was standing in the open doorway, looking ill at ease, as though unsure of his welcome. Was it the kiss? she thought suddenly. Had he regretted the impulse to show his support in such an intimate way? Or was he expecting her to be angry and bracing himself to apologize?

She felt her face warming at the thought of that very controlled mouth relaxing over hers again. His breath had been flavored with strong coffee and restraint, yet for the briefest instant his lips had clung hungrily to hers as though he'd been the one in need.

Her breath caught, then whooshed out in an embarrassing rush. It was silly to feel all warm and cozy inside at the memory of a single kiss. A kiss she hadn't been able to resent—or forget.

"Nobody home," she echoed, curving her lips into what she hoped was a composed smile.

"Someone special?" He raised one thick golden eyebrow. It was the one bisected by a scar and added a hint of wry humor to the rough-hewn face. It was a deadly combination of brooding intensity and hidden sensitivity that tempted a woman to take chances and ignore risks.

"My downstairs neighbor. I was hoping he could bring me my purse and a change of clothes from my apartment." She waved her hand to show him it wasn't important. "I'll try him again later."

He nodded and strode closer, bringing the scent of the outdoors into the small room. The rumpled look to his dark blue T-shirt and ragged jeans suggested he'd just come from the job site, as did the lines of weariness around his eyes. He needed a shave, she realized, and the dark blond stubble added rugged texture to an already unyielding jaw.

"How are you feeling?" he asked as he set a small brown paper bag in front of her on the bed tray.

"Psychedelic," she said, indicating the multicolored bruises surrounding both of her eyes. "Too bad it's not Halloween. I wouldn't have to rent a costume."

His mouth softened as though contemplating a smile that never came. "Give it a week and you'll be back to normal."

"I'll settle for presentable," she countered with a rueful smile that sent a sliver of pain into her right temple. "Ouch," she muttered, pressing two fingers gingerly against the now-throbbing spot, and held her breath until the ache eased.

Mindful of keeping her head perfectly still, she lifted her lashes and found him watching her. "Everyone keeps telling me I've got to be careful, but who'd think the simple act of smiling would be dangerous?"

"Depends on who's doing the smiling." His gaze flickered to her mouth and lingered until she felt her lips tingle and then part. He frowned then, and jerked his gaze to the door, as though looking for an escape.

Surely this intensely masculine man who'd been so utterly cool in an emergency couldn't be shy, she thought. Or could he? The thought both gave her pause and aroused her protective instinct.

"Would you...um, like to sit down?"

"Sure, I guess I can stay for a few minutes," he said, after taking what seemed like forever to think it over. He glanced around, then pulled the chair closer before settling into the seat.

"Is this for me?" she asked, touching the bag touting Mac and Joe's Famous Double-deckers. The thought of real food was making her mouth water.

"Yep. I figured you'd be pretty tired of hospital cuisine by now."

"You figured right," she admitted with a little laugh. "Four days of bland and boring is about my limit, even if it *is* good for Tory and me." Without bothering to hide her eagerness, she opened the bag and inhaled the wonderfully sinful aroma of hamburger grease.

"I hope you ordered it with everything," she said as she reverently lifted the foil-wrapped burger from the bag.

His eyes crinkled, lending an irresistible charm to his starkly male features. "Is there any other way?"

"Not in this lifetime," she said with a hearty sigh before taking a bite. "Ambrosia," she murmured when she'd chewed and swallowed.

The cheeseburger did indeed taste marvelous, but she couldn't help wishing she had a serving of sauerkraut to go with it. Followed by a double scoop of peppermint ice cream slathered in fudge sauce.

Conscious that Boyd was watching her more closely than she at first realized, she made herself finish the entire sandwich, even though her stomach was threatening to rebel. The last thing she wanted to do was appear ungrateful for his kindness. And it was a kindness, she realized as she blotted her lips with the napkin she'd found tucked neatly beneath the hamburger.

She wanted to tell him she understood how difficult this must be for him, given the loss of his wife and child, but she was hesitant to bring up a painful subject, especially since she'd heard the story from a third person.

"If I were a cat, I'd be purring big-time," she said instead, and hoped the smile she gave him expressed the depth of her appreciation.

"How's the little one?"

His question was casual, even offhand, but Stacy caught the flash of strong emotion in his gaze when it had rested briefly on her tummy.

"Actually she's been very quiet today." She tried for a light tone as she added, "Dr. Jarrod was telling me this morning about the good luck they've had here with preemies." Her hands trembled slightly as she returned the foil to the bag and crumpled both into a tight ball. "Of course, the odds would be more favorable if I could just make it into my ninth month."

Boyd heard the quaver in her voice, saw the sudden shimmer of tears in her eyes and wanted to bolt. Try as he might, he'd never quite managed to numb himself to the sights and sounds of another's suffering, which was just another reason why he made a better carpenter than doctor.

Uncomfortable and antsy, he shifted until he was resting one ankle on his knee. A few hours in that hard plastic chair could effectively wring a confession from a saint, he thought. And he was about as far from sainthood as any man could get.

"Jarrod is the best," he said, and meant it. "If anyone can keep that little one where she belongs for another month he can."

"Yes, so everyone here keeps telling me."

"But you don't believe it?"

She took a breath and straightened slender shoulders more suited to tailored silk than faded hospital cotton. "Yes, I believe it. I have to believe it. Otherwise…"

She took a breath, then another, clearly struggling for control. She did her best to blink back tears but there seemed to be too many.

He felt his mouth go dry. The quick, determined smile had him shoring up walls he'd thought invulnerable. Worse, he was strongly tempted to bundle her poor bruised body into his arms and hug her until she felt safe and reassured again. Only the memory of the last time he'd held a woman had him backing down hard.

"There should be a box of tissues around here someplace," she murmured, wiping her wet cheeks with her fingertips. Leaning forward, Boyd plucked one from the box on the small metal storage cabinet and handed it to her.

"Here, blow."

"I went to a psychic once, right after I graduated from college," she said between unladylike honks. "She told me I was an old soul, and therefore likely to be rather intense about things." Finished with the tissue, she tossed it into the nearby trash basket.

Boyd heard the clatter of dinner trays and realized he'd stayed far longer than he'd planned. Determined to say goodbye and mean it this time, he glanced at his watch and was about to make his polite farewells when the RN on duty walked in.

Built like a bean pole topped with straw, Maureen Schultz was as professional as they came—and as irreverent. Nothing was sacred to her—except human life. As a nurse, she had no equal. The same could be said about her tendency to be a pain in the butt.

Spying him sitting next to the bed, she broke into a teasing grin. "My stars, the reclusive Dr. MacAuley has actually graced the halls of PortGen with his presence again."

Even though her tone was light, he heard the unspoken questions. Was he still grieving? Still having nightmares? Still not returning phone calls from well-meaning friends?

"Still terrorizing the interns?" he inquired mildly as he got to his feet.

"Just the lazy ones." Grinning, she reached for the blood

pressure cuff in the wall holder. Widening her grin, she turned toward Stacy, who obediently held up her arm. "Would you believe this hulking brute was once the most promising resident we had on the surgical service?" she asked as she wound the cuff securely.

"I know he's cool in an emergency."

Boyd saw the quick look Schultz shot his way and gritted his teeth. Restless again, he ambled to the window and looked out on the parking lot. The mercury vapor lights cast an eerie blue aura over the cars lined up in their neat rows. How many of the visitors who had come in those cars had come to see near-strangers? he wondered. A half dozen, a couple? One?

So he had a soft spot in his cynical heart for a small, sleek woman with grit. No problem. Hell, he also had a soft spot for lonely little kids like Heidi. Who wouldn't? But, hey, he was a guy who pounded nails for a living, not a social worker.

When the job on Astoria was done, he'd move on to another job, and Heidi would find another "best friend" to jabber at when she was lonely. When Stacy's bruises were healed and her condition stable, she would go back to her world and out of his thoughts. When that happened, they would both be better off.

"Any contractions since the last time I was in?" he heard Schultz ask, and turned his gaze toward the bed in time to see Stacy's eyes cloud.

"A tiny one. More like a twinge."

"How long ago?" he asked, earning him another appraising glance from Schultz's laser-keen eyes.

"Two hours, more or less—" Stacy admitted, before adding too quickly, "—nothing to worry about, right?"

Boyd lifted a hand to the back of his neck, where a sudden knot had formed. "Like someone told me once, worry is the world's most useless emotion."

Finished with the pressure reading, Schultz removed the cuff before patting Stacy's shoulder. "He's right, Mrs. Patterson. What you need right now is rest."

"Seems like that's all I've done since I've been here."

The nurse smiled. "Don't fret about those cramps. It's probably just the baby settling down again."

Stacy smoothed the sheet over her tummy and wondered if Tory was awake or asleep. "I'll...try not to."

Nurse Schultz nodded once before shifting her attention to Boyd. "Dr. Ivans is retiring at the end of the year."

"Good for him."

Schultz folded her arms and cocked one hip. "Rumor has it he offered you a piece of his practice if you'd come back and finish your residency."

Lifting one eyebrow, he offered her a lazy smile. "Since when did a smart lady like you start listening to rumor?"

Stacy watched the nurse's thin chest expand in a sigh and empathized with the woman's frustration. Clearly Boyd MacAuley had a stubborn side that seemed as strong as his propensity for kindness.

"I give up," the nurse muttered before turning to Stacy again. "Is there anything you need?"

Stacy had a wild urge to rattle off the growing list, beginning with next month's rent money and ending about a hundred items later with a heartfelt plea for a hug.

"Nothing, thanks," she said instead, and summoned a grateful smile for all the woman and her colleagues had already done to make her stay a little less miserable.

"Just buzz if you think of something," the nurse said before leaving.

Boyd stood for a moment watching the empty doorway before he shifted his gaze to Stacy again. She had a way of looking at a man that tempted him to rest his head against those soft, womanly breasts and confess his deepest, darkest secrets.

"It sounds as though your decision to take a break from practicing medicine hasn't been received with universal joy," she said quietly.

"I didn't take a break. I quit."

"For good?"

"For the good of my patients."

Her gaze chided him gently. "I think you must have been a marvelous doctor."

Boyd felt something hard and hurting grind in his chest. He heard the sound of dinner trays sliding from the carts and the chatter of voices as the patients greeted the aids serving them. The aroma of food blended with the sharp medicinal odor that seemed to permeate the air, even in the downstairs lobby.

God, he hated this place. The sights, the smells. The guilt. His heart thudded and he felt a wild need to escape. He cleared his throat and managed what he hoped was a decent enough smile. "Well, take care of yourself."

"I'll do my best. And thanks for sneaking me some real food. It was heavenly." The eyes that were wide on his reflected understanding and concern and an open affection that shook him hard.

"No problem." He nodded, made another stab at a smile and left. Fast. By the time he'd made it to the elevator, he'd convinced himself he wouldn't be back.

# Five

Boyd woke with a start, his heart pounding and his body damp. Even with his eyes wide open, it took him a few seconds to realize he was in his own bedroom, sprawled facedown across his own bed with one arm hugging his pillow.

It was dark outside, though when he turned his head, he could get a glimpse of a nearly full moon through the open windows. A quick check of the clock showed that four hours had passed since he'd gone to sleep around midnight.

He didn't know when he'd started dreaming, or how long it had lasted. But he did know he'd been making love to Stacy Patterson in this particular dream. And, God help him, he was still distended and hot.

That in itself didn't surprise him, since he'd gone to bed thinking about her. Wondering if her body would feel as soft as it looked. Craving the feeling of her breasts flattening against his chest when he pulled her into his arms. Warm, soft breasts, perfectly formed with hard little tips he'd ached to suck. Breasts already swelling with milk, breasts that tasted sweeter with each lap of his tongue.

In his dream she'd moaned when he closed his mouth over her distended nipple. And when he'd lifted his head and looked at her face, her lush, pale lips had been curved in a drowsy smile and those incredible green eyes had been shimmering with a need as great as his own.

Remembering had a hot and aching need throbbing deeper and deeper until he could no longer lie still. The kind of need that goes beyond the physical to wrap around a man's soul until he longed to feel himself easing a part of himself into her forever.

He should have known better than to kiss her. Remembering the silk of her lips against his had him clenching his teeth and telling himself to think about something else. Anything but the taste of her. Anything but the longing to taste her again, each kiss more drugging than the last until he had to taste deeper. In his dream, her mouth had been vulnerable and hesitant at first, then opening eagerly to the first gentle thrust of his tongue. And then he had thrust deeper and deeper until her lips had closed around his probing tongue.

A groan escaped his lips, and he turned on his side, trying to ease the pressure in his loins. The friction of rigid flesh against the bedclothes only made it worse. Still tasting the kiss, he closed his eyes and forced himself to go to sleep.

For the first time since his rebellious teens Boyd overslept, so it was nearly seven-thirty by the time he stepped from the shower. Stalking across the hall into the bedroom, he made himself concentrate on the day ahead. As was his custom, he mentally rehearsed the details of the job one by one. By the time he'd cemented the plans for the day in his head, he was dressed, had jerked the quilt over the thrashed sheets and gulped down the pot of coffee he'd readied for brewing the night before.

A quick glance at his watch on the way to the kitchen told him to forget breakfast. Another glance after he'd rinsed his cup and put it in the drainer to dry promised he'd be at the job site by eight-fifteen, forty-five minutes late. Not bad, he assured himself firmly as he grabbed a banana from the bowl on the counter. No problem to make that up working late. A man couldn't build a decent reputation as a carpenter if he couldn't keep his customers happy. And if he couldn't make a living, he couldn't pay off the mountain of student loans that had gotten him through med school.

After his debts were settled, he intended to sell up and head south. To southern California, maybe, or Mexico. Someplace where it didn't rain nine months out of the year. Someplace where he didn't see reminders of all that he'd lost everywhere he went. Someplace where he could bake the chill out of his bones while he figured out how he was going to get through the rest of his life.

Mill Works Ridge seemed deserted as he exited the back door and headed for his truck. The rain had slacked off, but the sky was still black to the west, and the air had a raw, earthy scent. He was heading down the walk toward the carport when Prudy came hurrying out of her back door, dressed for the weather in a red slicker that made him think of Little Red Riding Hood.

As soon as she saw him, she veered in his direction. "I need a favor," she called without bothering with the usual pleasantries. He heard the tension in her voice, saw it, too, in her face and his heart began to thud faster. His first thought was of Stacy, his second was a cold fear.

"Problems?" He was surprised his voice was so calm, given the sudden tightening in his throat.

She took a fast breath. Her cheeks were flushed, and she hadn't bothered with makeup. "I'll say. A Greyhound skidded out of control and hit a stalled van on the 405."

Relief that it wasn't Stacy in peril was almost immediately replaced by a sick dread. "Casualties?" He knew the answer even before he'd asked. He only hoped the van hadn't been full of kids.

"Multiple, I understand. On the bus, primarily." She sighed. "Just my luck to be on call."

"Don't give me that. You would have gone anyway."

She flashed him an annoyed look. "Like you wouldn't?"

He cringed inwardly at the memory of the last time he'd

been on call. It had also been the last time he'd been in an OR. "What's the favor?" he asked more brusquely than he'd intended.

If Prudy noticed the tension in his voice, she gave no sign. Instead, she dug into the slicker's pocket and pulled out a folded slip of paper. "I promised Stacy Patterson I'd stop by her apartment and pick up some things for her."

"What happened to the downstairs neighbor?"

"Apparently she couldn't reach him," she said, shoving the paper into his hand. "Here's the address and the list of things she needs. Her apartment's the one on the second floor. Door's unlocked. Seems her wacko ex didn't even give her time to lock it before he dragged her out."

Boyd wanted to refuse. Instead, he shoved the paper into his back pocket and headed back down the walk with Prudy. "How's she doing?"

"As good as anyone can be in a situation like hers." Prudy frowned and offered him a frustrated look. "Her in-laws claimed their son's body yesterday, then spent a delightful half hour with Stacy, accusing her of driving their precious son to his death."

Boyd offered a succinct opinion of the elder Pattersons that had Prudy nodding in agreement. "Any idea when Jarrod plans to release her?" he asked as they reached their adjoining carports.

"Day after tomorrow, *if* her condition continues to improve."

*If*, he thought as he opened the door to Prudy's ancient Volvo for her. He sure as hell hated ifs.

The address was in the oldest section of town and looked it. The house in front was an ugly two-story brick the color of mud. The wood trim had been painted a sick pea green that was flaking off like dandruff, revealing a dull mustard undercoat. Without really trying, Boyd spotted three potentially dangerous structural cracks as he drove around to the rear.

What had once been a two-car garage with servants' quarters above was now a duplex of sorts, with one apartment up and one down. Between the house and the garage was a narrow patch of lawn with the scruffy look of long-term neglect. What grass had somehow managed to survive amidst the garbage cans and junked auto parts was a scraggly brown.

The crumbling driveway ended abruptly at the spot where a garage door had been inexpertly replaced by mismatched brick. Boyd parked close to a ramshackle fence and took the rickety steps leading to the upper apartment two at a time. At the top he found the mailbox stuffed full. Mostly fourth-class flyers and circulars addressed to "Occupant," he realized as he collected the lot to carry inside with him.

Just as Prudy had promised, the door was unlocked. Inside, he found one large room with a kitchen alcove at one end and what he took to be an enclosed bathroom at the other. An ironing board stood in one of the far corners along with a half-filled laundry basket. In the other was an old-fashioned wicker bassinet and a small white chest with wooden alphabet blocks for drawer pulls.

What light there was came from four small windows, one to a wall, and the place smelled of new paint layered over ancient mildew. In the distant past the walls had been painted a nondescript tan which had faded unevenly until the four walls had taken on the dreary look of water-damaged parchment, offset here and there by framed travel posters in vivid blues and greens. The furnishings were sparse and mismatched. Two chairs, one Naugahyde, one worn velour sat opposite a muddy brown sofa that apparently served as a bed. Draped over the back was a soft-looking afghan that reminded him of a rainbow.

After closing the door, Boyd walked toward the kitchen end, his heels echoing hollowly on the uneven wood floor. Roughly half of the cupboards had been neatly painted in bright yellow enamel, presumably from the gallon can still sitting on newspaper on the burn-scarred counter. A brush lay nearby, stiff now with paint and stuck to the newspaper on which it rested. It was the same color he'd seen on Stacy's clothes the day of the accident. And on her bruised cheek.

It had been so long since he'd felt anything it took him a

moment to realize he was touched by her brave attempt to brighten up her dreary surroundings. And damn if it wasn't working, at least as far as she'd gotten.

He had a hunch that given enough time and paint and imagination, she would have the place as sparkling and bright as a sunny day. Her own little cozy nest, he thought as he ran his gaze over the items on her list.

Only a kindergarten teacher would print the damned thing, and with perfectly formed letters that reminded him of dusty schoolrooms and endlessly boring afternoons when he'd longed to be outside in the sunshine. But then, his first teacher had had a voice like the seal she'd resembled and a tendency to rap his knuckles at the slightest sign of rebellion, while Stacy's voice was clear and surprisingly low for such a slight woman. And when it was flavored with a smile, it made him feel young and strong and eager to slay dragons for the woman he loved.

He knew better now. Some dragons were just too strong. For him, anyway.

He lifted his gaze and located a sad-looking bureau, a reject from a thrift shop if he'd ever seen one. A brown purse sat next to a framed photograph of a younger-looking Stacy in a bikini holding a fluffy white kitten with blue eyes.

He figured her for eighteen, nineteen at the most, in the first bloom of breathtaking beauty. Beneath delicately arching brows and framed by sooty lashes, her wide-set green eyes were sparking and alive and innocent. Her lips were rosy and slightly parted as though she'd been caught at the beginning of a laugh. Her nose was slightly crooked, and the dimple winking at the left side of her mouth gave her face an unbalanced look he found surprisingly appealing.

Her hair had been longer then and the glossy sun-tipped tendrils spread like a lush fan over her shoulders to end just above the swell of her breasts. Her body was trim and compact, and perfectly proportioned. Her skin was smooth, darkened by the sun to an enticing honey gold. It would feel like warm silk against a man's stroking hand, he thought, and then ground his teeth as his body stirred.

There was nothing posed or studied about the picture, nothing to suggest an attempt to appear provocative or sexy. Yet, she was both. Then and now. Just thinking about holding that small, soft body in his arms was enough to nudge his imagination toward the heated friction of skin against skin. And then what, MacAuley? Explain to her that you're only interested in sex? A fast and furious affair, followed by a faster goodbye and have a nice life. Now that would be a real class act, all right, especially after all she'd been through.

Disgusted with himself, he jerked open the top drawer to find panties and bras, plain as white bread. Yet the nunlike garments carried the faintest scent of flowers and spice. Intensely feminine yet subtly provocative, it was a fragrance that would appeal to a woman with secret fantasies and desires.

Or torment a man who'd been alone too long, he thought as he grabbed a set, then looked around for a suitcase. He found it on the top shelf of the closet and carried it to the sofa, one corner of which, he noted, was held up by a stack of well-thumbed paperback books.

After snapping open the case, he tossed in the undies, then returned to the dresser. Another quick search yielded a choice of nightgowns—one long and flannel and the other short, silky and trimmed with lace. He made a quick mental picture of her in both, a natural consequence—or was it a curse?—of male DNA, then chose the short one. Not because he was imagining the lush outline of her breasts beneath the thin material or visualizing the heavy lace brushing the sleek thighs indelibly imprinted on his mind, but because the weather was too hot for flannel. And, okay, just maybe because the skimpy nightie seemed like the perfect shade to bring out the gold in her eyes.

Hurrying now, he found a fuzzy white robe on a hook on the back of the bathroom door and whimsical tiger slippers nearby. While he was in the john, he collected the toiletries she'd specified and carried everything back to the suitcase. After checking the list one more time, he tossed her purse and the mail into the case and slammed it shut.

Warped by years of wet winters, the door to the outside was little more than a flimsy barrier against the elements, with no dead bolt or peephole. He pushed the button in the knob and stepped onto the landing, pulling the door shut behind him. After testing the lock, he started down the steps only to slow halfway down at the sight of a fat toad of a man peering suspiciously into the cab of his truck.

"Something I can do for you, friend?" Boyd called as he took the last steps with an easy stride that belied the sudden tension bunching the muscles of his thighs.

The man turned and raked him with hard black eyes set in liverish yellow. A couple of inches over six feet, with the look of a wrestler gone to seed, the guy reeked of sour sweat and cheap tobacco.

"This here your rig?" he demanded in a raspy, bottom-of-the-bottle voice.

"Must be, since it's my name on the registration."

After a moment's study, the man jerked his stubbled chin in the direction of a faded sign tacked to the wall to the left of Boyd's truck. "Like them words there say, this here lot's for tenants only."

"Sorry. I assumed this spot went with the upstairs apartment."

"It does. You don't."

"No problem, I'm leaving." Boyd set the suitcase in the truck's bed and opened the door to the driver's side.

"You a friend of Miz Patterson's?"

Boyd dug his keys out of his pocket. "Could be. Any reason why you need to know?"

"Yeah, I got a reason. I own this here place and I don't need nobody breaking in and stealing from my tenants, even them like Miz Patterson that ain't got much worth stealing."

Boyd gave some thought to the shabby rooms upstairs and Stacy's attempts to turn them into a home. She'd been lucky so far that some wandering junkie or strung-out kid hadn't tried the door and found it open. Luckier still the ass in front of him hadn't sold off what little she had, then reported it stolen.

"I'll tell Mrs. Patterson you were looking out for her," he

said when he'd leveled the need to lay out a few hard and fast rules for the man concerning his fragile tenant.

Oblivious to the sarcasm Boyd had infused into his voice—or maybe too drunk to notice—Stacy's landlord directed a pointed look toward the suitcase. "If you ain't stealing, how come you came down toting that?"

"Mrs. Patterson is in the hospital and needs some of her things."

"Got rid of that baby, did she?" The man snorted a laugh. "I figured she would, sooner or later."

"You figured wrong." Boyd rested both hands on his hips and reminded himself he'd left his brawling days behind. "Mrs. Patterson was injured in an auto accident."

"Don't surprise me none to hear it, what with the way her boyfriend peeled outta here. Crazy SOB damn near hit my truck, too. Had me half a mind to call the cops and report him."

Boyd felt his jaw clench. "Did you ever think Mrs. Patterson might be in trouble?"

The landlord shrugged. "I ain't no neighborhood watch."

"I'll be sure to pass along your good wishes when I see her again," Boyd drawled before he climbed behind the wheel.

The landlord's fleshy lips corkscrewed into a grin. "Yeah, sure. Why not? Right after you tell her the rent's still due on the first, accident or no accident."

"Your compassion is bottomless, I see." Boyd slammed the door while at the same time twisting the key to fire the engine.

Over the sudden roar, the man yelled something he didn't catch. "Nice talking to you, too," he yelled back before slamming the shift into reverse. He was actually disappointed when the bastard managed to get out of the way.

It was nearly six-thirty when Boyd stepped off the elevator across from the second floor nurses' station. He didn't recognize the woman in a pink smock busily entering something into a patient's computer record or the preppie kid with an intern's haggard face inhaling coffee from a large foam cup.

Boyd remembered his year as an intern—twelve months of

too much work and not enough sleep for a salary well below the poverty level. Instead of the satisfaction he'd expected after endless years of hard studying, rising hopes and the frustration of being a hick in the city, it had turned out to be hell itself. He hoped the kid had independent means to see him through—or a wife who was willing to pay more than her share of the bills. Like Karen.

Her money had come from her father who'd never forgiven Boyd for refusing the six-figure wedding present Kerwin Waverly had tried to settle on them. Not that Kerwin had honored his new son-in-law's wishes, of course. Instead, he'd simply opened an account in Karen's name.

Used to nice things and an indulgent daddy, she'd spent it for things Boyd hadn't been able to provide, things for the house and for herself, things he'd grudgingly decided he hadn't had the right or the heart to deny her. Even so, he'd had to suck in a harsh breath every time he'd come home, tired and hungry, and desperate to feel like a man in charge of his life instead of a robot with a scalpel, only to find she'd been shopping again.

He'd accepted title to the cottage on Mill Works Ridge because Karen had loved it on sight and because it and the other five dwellings had needed work Boyd himself could do as his own way of paying for the place, but he'd drawn the line when she'd offered to replace his ancient VW bug with a new sports model that didn't drink oil like water and stall more than it ran. After the funerals for Karen and the baby, he'd given the money he'd inherited to a local shelter for the homeless.

The door to Stacy's room was propped open, and he saw that she was out of bed and standing by the window looking out. It was the first time he'd seen her on her feet, which at the moment were bare except for an Ace bandage wrapping one ankle.

Though she was still too thin, her tummy had grown rounder in the week she'd spent in the hospital and her breasts seemed fuller beneath the voluminous hospital gown, reminding him of an alabaster fertility totem he'd seen in a magazine once.

His mind went again to the scrap of silk and lace he'd packed in the case. Before he could stop himself, he'd conjured up the image of the sleek gown molding to her ripe curves. He felt his body stir at the thought and cursed himself for the utter lack of respect for a woman who'd just been through a terrible ordeal.

Gritting his teeth, he rapped on the open door and saw her start. Averting her face, she quickly swiped her fingers over both cheeks and squared her shoulders before she turned away from the window to greet him. Her bruises had faded, but those unforgettable eyes were still haunted with worry and her skin was too pale. Even so, she held her thin shoulders proudly, as though daring the world to try to knock her down again.

"I've been watching a hummingbird in that red rose of Sharon by the light pole," she told him with a smile. "She must have a nest hidden in the leaves because she won't let any other bird get any closer than ten feet or so. She goes into this dive-bombing frenzy, swooping and screeching and flapping those little bitty wings like helicopter rotors. A few minutes ago she even scared off this huge jay, though heaven only knows what she would have done if that big guy had called her bluff."

Fight like hell, he thought. Like a small, pale woman with fire in her soul. He cleared his throat and answered her smile with one of his own. "What's Dad's part in this scuffle?"

She glanced once more through the pane, then shook her head. "I have a feeling mama hummingbird is single parent."

"There's a lot of that going around," he said, crossing to the metal locker by the bathroom door.

"Hey, that looks like my suitcase," she exclaimed with a wide-eyed look that didn't quite hide the swollen lids and damp lashes.

"Probably because it is," he said, stashing the suitcase inside. "Your purse and mail are in the case."

"You went with Prudy to my apartment? To get my things?" A wisp of a frown settled between her dark eye-

brows, and he felt a quick pang of guilt. As though he'd somehow done something wrong.

"Prudy had to work. She asked me to help her out." He
shut the locker door and stepped back. "It's all there, everything on the list."

Stacy expressed her thanks and thought about those large,
capable, very masculine hands rummaging through the bras
and panties no other man had touched or even seen, just as no
other man had touched her swollen belly. Remembering the
gentleness with which he'd comforted in those awful minutes
after the accident had a fresh wash of tears coming to her eyes.

"Damn, I swore I wouldn't do this," she muttered, squeezing her eyes shut, but the tears kept coming, like a dam over-
flowing.

Boyd didn't know what else to do, so he lifted a hand to
brush away the tears. Her skin felt like warm, wet silk beneath
the pads of his fingers. Need speared through him, as sharp as
pain. "Stacy..." His voice ended on a jagged moan as he gave
in to that need and took her mouth. He felt her tremble, felt
her fit her mouth more closely to his.

Knowing he shouldn't, yet driven beyond his ability to resist, Boyd widened his stance, drawing her against the length
of his body until her rounded belly was snuggled against his
and her soft warm breasts were pressed sweetly against his
chest. She fit, as though she belonged in his arms, and that
realization had hard, painful knots forming in his gut.

At the same time, with each long, drugging kiss, with every
eager little sound she made, he felt reborn, alive to the heady
taste of a woman's kiss. His head was swimming, his thoughts
tumbling. She wasn't his wife or his lady, or even someone
he knew well.

But, God help him, she tasted sweet and her lips were welcoming soft. Somehow she'd gotten to him in a way no other
woman ever had—her eyes, her smile, the determined tilt of
that small chin as she took on a mountain of problems.

He could handle that, even offer his help. It was the near
savage need to ease her back onto the hard hospital bed and

slowly strip the gown from her ripening body that had him drawing back. It wasn't a lover she needed, but a friend.

Cupping her shoulders, he eased her from him until her belly was no longer touching his. Head swimming, his lungs laboring to draw enough air, he struggled to clear his mind. He knew his face was flushed as he watched her sway, then slowly flutter her long lashes open. Her lips were still parted, rosy now instead of pale, and her green eyes were slightly dazed as they fastened on his.

"Who was that masked man?" she murmured, her tone a little breathless, a little bemused.

Boyd took a breath and put together a string of words in his head, tested them for the proper blend of humor and respect. When they seemed to work okay, he tried on his best doctor-to-patient smile. "Stacy, I—"

"Don't say it, please."

"Don't say what?" he questioned, mentally stiffening the wall that always seemed in danger of toppling around this woman.

"That the magic that happened between us just now was a mistake, because it wasn't."

Boyd had enough control left to keep from reaching for her again. "Maybe not, but it sure as hell isn't going to happen again."

"Why not?"

"Because it's wrong, that's why. I know how much it hurts to lose someone...." He took a breath and struggled to put words to things he only half understood. "Your in-laws visiting and all, you have to be thinking of Tory's father, maybe wishing he was the one you were kissing..."

"I know who I was kissing, Boyd. I won't insult you by asking that same question of you."

The splash of hurt in her eyes had him grinding his back teeth and cursing himself for the inarticulate country boy he was at heart. "Don't look at me like that, Stacy. I'm trying to do the right thing here. The decent thing."

It wasn't working, he realized, plowing his hand through his hair. The hurt was still there, along with a vulnerability around her mouth. "You've just been through a hell of a bad time. You're scared, and you're vulnerable."

"And you felt sorry for me." Her chin came up and she smiled. "That *is* what you're trying to say, isn't it?"

He bit back a need to tell her that "sorry" was the last thing on his mind. "That's just it, Stacy. I don't feel. It's the way I like it. The way it has to be."

"I think you feel very deeply. Too deeply. And I think you felt something just now when you kissed me."

He felt heat climbing his neck. He was immune to damn near every wile a woman possessed—everything but the unguarded look of longing in the eyes of a woman who believed in fortune-tellers. "Stacy, I'm not the hero you see in your mind."

She reached up to touch his face and he flinched. Sadness flickered in her eyes, but she curved her lips into a forgiving smile. "What I *see* is a very kind, very decent man I care about very much."

"Damn it, Stacy, haven't you been listening to me? I can't give you what you need from the man in your life. I can't give you anything but grief." He realized he was close to shouting and hauled in hard on the need to vent his frustration any way he could. Before he could change his mind, he turned on his heel and left.

# Six

"**D**amn thing's still lopsided," Boyd muttered, standing back with clippers in hand to study the result of a good four hours' work. The hedge that had started out shoulder high had been whittled to a manageable three feet, its top as flat as a landing strip. Sighting down the length, he saw ripples and dents that shouldn't be there. It was even worse on Prudy's side where those fat, fussy flowers she liked so much were smashed up against the privet bushes like pink and blue snowballs.

What had Stacy called them? Hydrangeas?

He eyed the lacy blossoms with a scowl and tried not to think about soft pink lips curved into a surprised smile that warmed and gentled.

The words he bit off came straight from his rebellious days hanging out in loggers' bars in the small mountain town where he'd grown up. The crude curse didn't help. He still felt lousy.

Seeing where Stacy lived, touching her things, had pushed him across a line toward an intimacy he didn't want. Couldn't handle even if he'd wanted it.

Hadn't he spent three years avoiding personal entanglements? Damn straight, he had. And he was good at it, an expert. His life was predictable, his decisions limited by his own choice. The only responsibilities he accepted revolved around his work. If he made a mistake and underbid a job, he absorbed the loss with a philosophical shrug and moved on to the next job. If he underestimated the time it would take him to complete a project, he worked extra hours without pay to bring it in on time. If he made a mistake—any mistake—*he* paid the price, no one else.

He didn't want a woman in his life, especially a woman with bruised green eyes and a kissable mouth. He didn't want to admire her spirit or worry about her living alone in a flimsy firetrap. Damn it, he didn't want to find her attractive or sexy or intriguing. And he sure as hell didn't want to dream about her again.

It was too easy to care about a woman when she was always on his mind, too easy to feel close to a woman who crowded his dreams so intimately he woke up hard and hungering. A man made lousy decisions when he let his body control his mind. He sure as hell had made his share.

Twenty minutes and a gallon of sweat later, he had reached the end of the edge closest to the carports and was about to call it a day when he heard Prudy's twenty-year-old Volvo wagon pull into the slot to the right of his.

Leave it to Boyd to do yard work on one of the hottest days on record, Prudy thought as she reluctantly left the car's air-conditioned coolness. But then, Boyd wasn't one to make things easy on himself.

She wanted to tell him it wouldn't help. The memories would still be there when he'd pushed his body to the point of exhaustion and his mind to numbness. Memories he couldn't outwork or outrun or bury deep enough. Memories he had to conquer if he was ever going to heal.

"I swear I'm giving my notice first thing tomorrow," she declared after slamming the car door behind her. "Even pounding nails for you would be more satisfying than baby-sitting drunks in the ER."

"What do you mean, *even?*" Boyd challenged, straightening slowly in deference to the tired muscles of his back.

Grinning, she sidestepped the wheelbarrow piled with clippings and joined him on the grass, her gaze sweeping back along the geometrically straight line of greenery. "I love you dearly, Boyd, but as a boss, you would be a nightmare."

"Gee, I guess that means you won't be asking me to help you remodel your kitchen."

She blew a strand of hair off her damp forehead. "Have I asked for your help?"

"You didn't have to. I remember the deck you put in last year. Correction, the deck *I* put in—after you'd damn near sliced off a foot with the power saw you borrowed from me."

Snorting, Prudy picked up a truncated pink blossom and looked at it with forlorn eyes. "I hope Stacy's not expecting another bouquet, because it looks like you haven't left flowers enough to fill even a bud vase."

Boyd felt heat climbing his neck. He should have gotten the damn flowers from a florist. "How's she doing?" he asked offhandedly. It had been two days since he'd seen her. And two damned nearly sleepless nights spent prowling his house in a rotten humor.

Prudy tucked the flower behind her ear and offered him a bland smile. "I imagine she's fine—or will be, once she lands a job."

"What?"

"She's been calling on the want ads, trying to find work. Last I heard, she hadn't come up with anything more solid than a few maybes."

Boyd thought about the bright yellow paint covering scarred dingy cabinets and a woman who was determined to brighten her life any way she could. "She didn't say anything to me about looking for work," he muttered, scowling at the mental image of Stacy on a rickety ladder, her balance made precarious by a full-blown pregnancy, determined to finish the job she'd started.

Prudy glanced down, hiding a smile. "Why? Do you have a job to offer?"

Boyd grunted, then bent to gather his tools. Stacy Patterson needed a keeper, he thought. Someone to watch over her until that baby she was so crazy about was delivered safely.

"If you're planning to visit her in the hospital, don't," Prudy said as he straightened to glare at her. "Jarrod released her yesterday morning."

Twenty-five minutes later Boyd pulled into the spot next to the familiar Tenants Only sign and vaulted up the steps to Stacy's apartment. Then, taking a deep breath, he lifted a fist and knocked. When she didn't answer, he knocked louder and longer before, giving in to a growing worry, he tried the knob and found the door locked tight.

"Stacy? Open the door. It's Boyd."

An angry—and definitely male—voice shouted a muffled obscenity an instant before the door was jerked inward. The man standing there was scrawny, unshaven and bleary-eyed. Boyd judged his age as mid-twenties, and his origin, when he spoke, deeply Southern.

"Hey, man, whatever you're sellin', I ain't interested." He started to close the door, but Boyd stiff-armed it open again.

"Where's Mrs. Patterson?" Deciding he didn't have the time or patience for a lengthy discussion, Boyd let an echo of his ill-spent adolescence slip into his voice.

"Hell if I know." The man cut his gaze toward the dun-colored house. "Ask the bastard yonder. He's the one who rented me this dump yesterday noon."

Boyd took a hard and fast hold on his temper. "What about Mrs. Patterson's clothes and the baby's things?"

The puzzled look in the kid's bloodshot eyes was all the answer Boyd needed. "Go back to sleep," he shot over his shoulder as he headed down the steps two at a time. By the time he got to the bottom the landlord was already on his way out of his back door. Boyd waited, his temper lashed tight.

"I thought that was your rig, cowboy." The man was spoiling for a fight. Boyd gave some thought to obliging him—after he'd gotten what he wanted from the hustler.

"Name's MacAuley. What's yours?"

The man's weasel eyes narrowed at Boyd's polite tone. "Wattchel. Not that it's any of your damned business."

"Well, I'll tell you, Mr. Wattchel," Boyd said slowly, carefully, rationing his words. "I was mostly raised by my grandmother, and she was a stickler for manners. Now she didn't believe in fighting unless a man had no other choice. She also believed it wasn't polite to beat the crap out of someone until you'd been properly introduced."

Wattchel's jaw went slack, then tightened around a foul curse. "You and what army?"

Boyd reminded himself that he could be patient in a good cause. "Mrs. Patterson's forwarding address. Get it now."

Wattchel's answer was crude and anatomically graphic. Boyd decided he wasn't all that patient after all. "Ah hell, Watchell, just when we were getting along so well." Before the big man could react, Boyd had him pushed up against the truck with a forearm jammed against the man's larynx. "Where did she go when you kicked her out?"

The landlord stared at him goggle-eyed, his lips pulled back in a rictus of fury. "I don't know what the hell you're talking about. I run a business here, not a charity. The lady knew my rules right up-front. Rent gets paid on time, period. I can't afford no grace period like them fancy places in Lake Oswego."

*"Where... is... she?"* Boyd exerted just enough pressure on the esophagus to guarantee the man's total attention. When panic surfaced in the man's eyes, Boyd eased off.

"Budget Motel on Eastern," Wattchel got out on a rush of foul-smelling air.

Boyd stepped back and lowered his arm. Because he'd been undersize and skinny until he was halfway through high school, he'd always favored a left to the gut and a right uppercut to the jaw in rapid-fire succession. He pegged Wattchel as a brawler with brute strength and no finesse.

He was right. Wattchel swung from the heels, his massive fist aimed at Boyd's nose. Expecting the blow, Boyd ducked easily, even as he felt his own fist thud into Wattchel's blubbery belly. But it was the solid smash of fist against jaw that sent an icy satisfaction shooting through his veins.

Wattchel went down like an axed log, his mouth open and

gasping, his eyes glazing over. Boyd took a minute to make sure the bastard was simply stunned before heading for his truck. It was only when he gripped the steering wheel that he realized he'd split three of the knuckles on his right hand.

In spite of the nervous churning in her stomach, Stacy knew she had to eat, for Tory's sake as well as her own. But after paying cab fare from the hospital to her apartment and then to the motel after her humiliating argument with her idiot landlord, she didn't even have enough money left for a carton of milk.

Tired of pacing the dreary room that was almost as hot and steamy as a sauna, she sank down on the lumpy bed and tried to think. As of this moment she had a roof over her head, a suitcase of clothes and the bottle of prenatal vitamins Boyd had brought her—along with a bill for her hospital expenses well into five figures.

Compared to that, the motel room was a steal. Which is exactly what it would be if she didn't come up with some cash and fast. So far, however, she hadn't even scrounged up a decent chance at landing a job. Much as it galled her, she was going to have to apply for assistance. But that would have to wait until Monday. The welfare office wasn't open on Sunday.

In the meantime—

The thud of a hard fist on the door startled her. In a panic, she shot a fast look around, but the shabby room had only one entrance and no telephone.

"Who is it, please?" she called, her hand automatically cupping her belly.

"It's Boyd, damn it. Let me in."

Surprise made her heart speed. Relief made her giddy. "I don't know any Boyd Damnit," she called as she unbolted the door.

The man on the other side was not laughing. Not even smiling. In fact, from the thunder in his eyes and the hard compression of his mouth, he was one breath shy of furious.

"What are you doing here?" she asked in a rush that deepened his frown.

"Getting you the hell out."

She offered a frown to match his. "How did you know I was here?"

"Wattchel."

"You went to my apartment?" It was a silly question. How else could he have known where to find her. There was another, more urgent question, however. "Why?"

"Damned if I know."

"Boyd—"

"Get your things." He bit off the words with those same hard lips.

"But—"

"Don't argue with me, Stacy. I'm not in the mood." He moved past her so fast she had to step backward to get out of his way. With an economy of movement that amazed her for so large a man, he had the few things she'd unpacked shoveled into her open suitcase and the suitcase itself closed almost before she could blink.

"Let's go." His voice had an edge sharp enough to slice nails.

"Go where, exactly?" Because she was feeling vulnerable and scared, Stacy planted her feet wider and lengthened her backbone.

"To find you another apartment."

She thought of her empty bank account and nudged her chin higher. "That's not necessary," she said stiffly.

He drew his eyebrows together. "You can't stay here."

"Why not? It's clean."

He dismissed that with a look. "Don't you read the papers? There've been two murders and at least one rape in this neighborhood already this year."

She knew the statistics all too well. But beggars, as some street-corner philosopher had once claimed, couldn't be choosers. They could, however, hang on to their self-esteem—or what was left of it. "I'll be careful."

He muttered something under his breath before disappearing into the bathroom. Two seconds later he reappeared carrying her small clutch of toiletries, which he threw into the open suitcase.

"Now listen here, Boyd MacAuley, those are my worldly possessions you're treating so cavalierly."

Ignoring her protests, he slammed the case shut and snapped the lock. "You're not staying here, period."

Telling himself it wouldn't do any good to snap at her, he carried the suitcase outside to his truck and tossed it into the bed. Returning to the room, he nodded impatiently toward the open door.

"Ready?"

Stacy took a breath. "Boyd, I appreciate your wanting to help, but I've imposed on you enough for one lifetime."

"Stubborn as a little mule," he muttered a split second before scooping her into his arms.

Stacy didn't know whether she wanted to sock him one on that hard jaw or snuggle down into his protective warmth. Because she couldn't decide, she settled for calling him a bully and brute.

He spared her an amused glance from dark gray eyes before turning toward the door. "My purse," she all but shouted when she realized she was leaving, like it or not.

He detoured to the dresser and allowed her to grab her bag and a deep breath before carrying her to the truck. Moments later, he had her belted into the passenger's seat and was himself behind the wheel.

"Wait," she blurted when he reached for the ignition key. "I, um, haven't paid for the room."

He glanced her way before shrugging. "I took care of it when I checked with the manager to get your room number. You can pay me back later."

Later? As in next week? A month from now? How long did it take to process a welfare application? she wondered, cringing inside.

"I need the receipt," she said with a smile she intended to look assertive. It felt stiff instead.

Without a word, he shifted to his left hip while using his right hand to pluck his wallet from the back pocket of his jeans. She noticed then that his knuckles were covered with dried blood.

Prodded by a need she didn't fully understand, she reached out to touch the discolored skin. He froze, his gaze instantly on hers.

"What happened?" she questioned softly.

His jaw tightened, as though he had suddenly gritted his teeth. "Ran into a door at your apartment."

Stacy had a sudden image of that same callused hand knotting into a huge, punishing fist, smashing into Griff Wattchel's Neanderthal jaw. She felt a moment of giddy elation, followed by a pang of conscience. No doubt about it, Wattchel was a pig, but to be fair, he had warned her up-front about paying the rent on time. So why had she thought he would make an exception in her case?

"Does it hurt?"

"Only when I laugh," he said with just the slightest softening of those hard lips, as though a smile were waiting.

"I'm sorry," she murmured, allowing her fingertips to caress the swollen flesh. She shouldn't be touching him, she realized when the quick flash of sympathy melted into something more elemental. More threatening. Something very close to love. Too close.

Boyd told himself he was glad when she drew back her hand. Told himself he was only thinking of her well-being. And the baby's. Told himself he didn't miss the sweet comfort of her hand on his.

Scowling, he flipped open his wallet and extracted the receipt she'd requested. "One receipt," he said, dropping it between them on the seat.

"Thank you."

"Welcome." He replaced his wallet before starting the engine. Now where? he thought. His proud little damsel had gotten herself out on a limb so thin the first wisp of breeze could snap it in two. She'd fall face first, too, before she'd ask for help. But like it or not, she was going to get it.

# Seven

Stacy watched the digital display on the dashboard clock tick off another minute. Sixteen had already passed since they'd left the Budget Motel, mostly in silence. At first, Stacy had tried small talk about the weather, Boyd's work, the heavier-than-usual Sunday traffic. Boyd had replied politely, in monosyllables, as though preoccupied. Finally she'd given up. After all, it was his truck, his rules.

Instinct told her that Boyd MacAuley wasn't the kind of man to impose his will on anyone. So why, suddenly, was he trying to take over her life? Frowning, Stacy shifted her gaze just enough so that she could study him through half-closed eyes. Boyd MacAuley, doctor turned carpenter, she thought. A loner with a heart of gold hidden behind a lot of walls. A formidable combination. An impressive man.

He made her nervous, and yet he made her feel safe. A stranger in the ways society counted relationships, yet she felt as though she'd known him forever. As though she could trust him implicitly. Could count on his steady strength and quiet reliability.

Yet, she was suddenly afraid to be alone with him. Not in the way she'd been afraid of Len, she knew, but in ways that were perhaps more dangerous. Ways that she couldn't control. Ways that had her feeling bursts of excitement whenever she thought of kissing him again.

Mistake, Stacy. Don't think about that. And for heaven's sake, do not, repeat, do *not* start weaving a romantic fantasy around two kisses and a hungry look in solemn charcoal eyes.

"Are you okay?" Boyd's deep voice was burred with a rough male concern that she found utterly endearing.

"Fine. Just a little sleepy." She was used to frequent naps in the hospital. That, too, would have to change when she landed a job. Tomorrow, she thought firmly. Even if she ended up flipping hamburgers.

"If it gets too cold in here, let me know and I'll turn down the AC."

"No, the cool air feels good."

Boyd spared her a quick look before returning his attention to the road ahead. Closing her eyes, she gave in to the weariness dragging her down. Only when the truck slowed, then changed direction did she open her eyes again.

Blinking away the fog in her brain, she sat up straighter and looked around. They were on a street in a neighborhood she'd never seen before, near the Columbia, she realized after a moment. On a bluff of some kind, with the river slipping quietly past below. It was quieter here, more small town than big city.

"Where are we?" she asked when Boyd slowed for an intersection.

"Mill Works Ridge."

He checked the traffic, then turned onto a tree-lined street that appeared to parallel the river. On the left was a park with a children's playground. On the right was a row of pretty frame bungalows. Though she could see a similarity in basic structure, each house had its own personality and charm. Stacy decided she would be happy living in any of them, and then dismissed the thought with a small sigh. It would be a long time before she could afford anything more than a small apartment.

"There used to be a mill where the River Watch shopping center is now," Boyd continued when he noticed her looking around. Her eyes, when she brought her gaze to his, were clear green in the sunshine, framed by lashes tipped with pure gold. "Old Chester Waverly built about two dozen houses along this street for some of his employees. Only six are left now."

Waverly? Stacy frowned, trying to remember where she'd heard that name before. From Prudy, she realized after a moment's concentration. When they'd been talking about Boyd's wife.

*She was a Waverly.*

Biting her lip, she sneaked a suspicious look in Boyd's direction. "I don't see any apartment houses," she said when he turned his head her way. Behind the aviator sunglasses, his eyebrows were drawn into a bold vee, and his jaw was bronzed steel, textured by the hint of a beard.

"This neighborhood's zoned single family."

"Does one of those houses happen to be yours?"

"It does."

Stacy drew a breath against the quick fluttering of her heart. "Is that where we're headed?"

"It is." One corner of his mouth flattened, and she thought she detected a faint wash of added color along the defined line of his cheek.

She frowned and looked down at her hands. "Funny, I don't remember accepting your gracious invitation to visit."

He glanced her way again, his eyes crinkling behind the dark lenses. "Don't expect four stars." He hesitated, scowled. "Three might even be a stretch."

Stacy fought a grin. He was having second thoughts about galloping full speed to her rescue, and now he was trying hard to figure out what to do next with the destitute widow. Poor Boyd, she thought. More generous than he wanted to be. And about the best man she'd ever known.

"Sorry, three stars is my downside limit," she said, watching him shift his gaze her way. "You'll just have to take me back to the motel."

Boyd saw the laughter sparkling like river water in her eyes and felt something tear inside him. Damn woman had been slammed around hard by an army of trouble, and yet she could still laugh. He, pathetic excuse for a man that he was, hadn't laughed in years. Really laughed. Hell, no, he'd been feeling too damned sorry for himself for that, he thought, returning his gaze to the road ahead.

A sudden tangle of emotions made him wish he'd put all of his weight into the uppercut he'd delivered to Wattchel's jaw. Maybe then he wouldn't be feeling like such a loser.

"Sorry," he told her, his voice rasped by feelings he neither wanted nor could banish, "this taxi only goes one way."

Her laugh was soft, almost sad. "At least it doesn't smash into trees."

"Bad memories?"

"Some."

From the corner of his eye he saw her rub a hand over her belly, then linger caressingly. He felt his breath catch and jerked his gaze back to the road.

"I read someplace that time tends to soften a lot of sharp edges," she murmured after a moment's silence.

And hones others to a razor's deadliness, Boyd thought, slowing for the turn into the driveway he shared with Prudy. He parked next to Prudy's Volvo and shut off the engine.

Glancing toward Stacy, he saw her take a quick, nervous look around before fixing her gaze on his. "Nurses do it in shifts," she said, offering a fleeting smile.

"Pardon?"

"The bumper sticker. On the Volvo." Her smile returned, steadier this time. "Prudy's, I assume."

Boyd nodded. So she felt safer with him knowing that Prudy was next door. Good thing she didn't have access to his thoughts—or his dreams—he decided as he climbed from the truck.

Stacy took a deep breath before unlatching her seat belt. The day's events had taken their toll, and she moved clumsily, exhaustion hovering oppressively, like the heat of the day. She longed for a long, cold drink and a nap, yet she knew she couldn't allow herself to settle into Boyd's house for more than a short stay. Anything longer would be charity, chipping away a large chunk of her pride. As it was, she had precious little left.

Fatigue, coupled with her weakened ankle and added bulk, made her clumsy, and she had trouble exiting the truck. Before she could find solid footing on the running board, Boyd muttered something she didn't catch.

"Pardon?" she murmured a split second before his hands bracketed her rib cage and she found herself being lifted free of the seat. His grip was strong, his fingers warm where they splayed intimately against her body, his blunt fingertips pressing only an inch or so beneath the swell of her breasts.

For an instant they were eye to eye. His were deep gray shot with flecks of silver and as dark as a gathering storm. And his mouth, so close to hers, was soft enough to make her own tingle. One corner curled upward a fraction, then froze as he let her down gently. Distracted, she hadn't thought to take her weight on her good ankle, and she cried out as pain shot like a tongue of searing flame along her calf.

Instantly she was in his arms again, pressed against the solid muscle and bone of his wide chest. His deeply tanned throat smelled of soap and a strong pulse was surging in the triangular hollow framed by the soft collar of his knit shirt. He said something about stupidity, his own mostly, and set off toward the house, his strides long and sure, his jaw suddenly hewn from granite.

He carried her easily, his breathing scarcely changing. The temptation to nestle into his sheltering warmth was close to irresistible. And dangerous. It would be far too easy to let herself depend on his strength while hers was at such a low ebb. And far too easy to let herself care deeply about him.

The word "love" floated for an instant in her consciousness, sending an electric thrill racing through her. Impossible, she protested silently. She was confusing gratitude with... affection. It was a common dynamic. Boyd had been there when she'd felt most alone and frightened, his big, rough hand holding hers tightly, his callused, muscular palm reassuring against hers. She'd felt so safe. So protected. *Adored.*

She blinked. Stiffened. She was veering way too close to fantasy again. And longing. "I can walk," she protested against his well-padded shoulder.

"Shut up." His voice approximated a growl, yet she sensed that his anger was directed inward. Frustration, she decided. She'd had enough of her own in the past to recognize the signs.

Only six more weeks to go until Tory was born—if luck was with her. She sighed again and tried to ignore the dull ache in her right temple. The headaches that had plagued her in the hospital had lessened in frequency but not in severity. Rest and quiet, Dr. Jarrod had ordered. And no stress. He hadn't mentioned how she was to accomplish that on the forty-five cents in her wallet.

By the time Boyd climbed the three steps to the back porch, she had herself under rigid control. He shifted, one arm tightening around her, while he managed to insert the key in the lock.

She felt his muscles flex and tighten and thought again of the wide bronze chest pelted by dusty blond hair she'd seen through the window of the Trans Am. Odd what details the mind selects to retain, she thought as he opened the door. Like the shift and flash of emotion in devil-dark eyes when his gaze turned her way. Or the subtle shimmering tension deep within her that curled deeper with each touch of his hand, each slow, bittersweet smile that did little to erase the sadness in his eyes.

Inside, the house was blessedly cool, a respite from the harsh glare of the sun. She had an impression of yellow walls and white appliances as he carried her through the kitchen and into the living room. Gently, and with an amazing lack of effort, he deposited her on a cushiony sofa the color of oatmeal, his hands sliding free of her body slowly, as though he were reluctant to let her go. She nearly gasped aloud at the shiver that passed through her when his work-hardened palms created a friction heat.

"Stay put while I get your things," he ordered, his expression so forbidding she wondered if she'd only imagined the soft cast to his mouth. "Then we'll negotiate." He turned and strode out of the room before she could wrap her mind around a suitable answer.

Negotiate what? she wondered with a sigh that seemed to come all the way from her toes. A deal? A loan? Your place or mine?

His, obviously, but only for the moment, she thought with a tired grin, glancing around. She'd expected…what? Clutter? Mismatched furniture? A man's lair? *Three stars might be a stretch.*

Instead, her surprised gaze took in a serene oasis of dusty blue and soothing cream, with touches of steel gray and mauve. A room bordering on classic elegance, even in so small a house. Everywhere she looked, she saw perfection—silver candlesticks so heavy and ornate they had to be antique and probably priceless, plush pile carpets, framed prints bearing flamboyant signatures and the discreetly penciled numbers of limited editions.

A glossy, glitzy setting for a man who came home with sawdust in his hair, and one, she realized sadly, that must have been created by his wife. The ghost Prudy had mentioned once.

Feeling awkward and out of place in a room worthy of a magazine spread, Stacy imagined Karen MacAuley as a slender woman with a graceful carriage gliding serenely through life, her blond hair in artful disarray and her blue eyes mirroring the haughty confidence that beauty and breeding inevitably bestow. A rich man's daughter. A doctor's wife. As perfect as the room she'd created. Yet, in the end, none of that mattered.

Stacy felt a pang of sympathy for the woman she would never know. And for the lonely man who had kept her house exactly as she must have left it.

Closing her eyes, she allowed herself to remember the empty days and restless nights she'd spent after the doctors had gently but firmly told her that the man she'd loved and married was gone forever. As dead as if he'd been in his grave instead of imprisoned in a madness that had turned him into a potentially lethal stranger.

Her friends had been there for her then, fellow teachers, wives of Len's brother officers. Prodding her to work through the stages of grief one by one. Supporting her when she cried, holding her when she screamed out her rage, listening with endless patience while she sorted through her memories of the golden years with Len, taking each one out like a precious gem, needing only to be polished to shine and shimmer again.

According to Prudy, Boyd had simply closed down inside. A man paying penance for surviving by living out the remainder of his life without joy. Without love.

Stacy frowned, sending a sudden stiletto strike into her temple. Pain exploded in one star-burst flash, before settling into an agonizing hammering. Biting her lip to keep from moaning, she fumbled in her purse for the bottle of mild painkillers Dr. Jarrod had insisted on prescribing—after she'd forced him to spend a good twenty minutes convincing her that they wouldn't have an adverse affect on Tory.

Her vision was wavering in and out with each pulsing pain, making it difficult to concentrate on the childproof top. Frustrated and fighting a sudden nausea, she closed her eyes, hoping to clear the cottony veil, then opened them with a snap when a strong male hand closed over hers. Preoccupied, she hadn't heard Boyd returning.

"Damn it, Stacy, why didn't you sing out for me?" His tone was gruff, but she heard the underlying panic. He was afraid for her. Squinting upward, she tried to smile but winced instead. His face paled, revealing freckles buried under the tan.

"Are you in labor? How far apart—"

"Headache," she whispered.

Boyd muttered something rude, then apologized. A twist of his powerful wrist and the cap came free. Just like that, she thought sourly.

"The…man who invented…those blasted caps…ought to be skinned alive," she declared between the sledgehammer blows bent on shattering her skull.

Boyd read the dosage aloud, then shook out the prescribed two tablets into one broad palm. "How do you know it was a man?'' he asked as he recapped the bottle before tossing it next to her on the cushion.

"Has to be.''

He grunted and reached for her hand. Turning it palm up, he slid the pills from his palm to hers, then gently folded her fingers over the tiny white tablets. "Hold on to these while I get you some water.'' Trapped by the pain, Stacy let her eyes drift closed and did as she was told.

When he returned, Boyd found her sitting perfectly still, her face chalk white with pain, her lips clamped tight. His breathing turned ragged, his fury at Luke Jarrod riding close to the surface. Damn man should never have discharged her, no matter how much pressure the damn insurance company laid on him.

"Stacy, open your hand, honey.'' It took some doing to keep his anger out of his voice. Later, when he was face-to-face with Jarrod, he'd let it loose but good.

He felt a slam in his gut when he saw how badly her fingers were shaking. She was hurting big-time, but at least she wasn't having contractions. "Put these in your mouth,'' he ordered softly when he'd taken the pills from her.

Obediently she parted her lips for him, her long, mink-colored lashes fluttering over eyes gone dull from the pain. Carefully he fed her the pills, watching to make sure they stayed on her tongue before he brought the glass to her lips. She drank deeply, her small hand wrapping his wrist as though to steady herself.

"Finish it,'' he urged when she drew back.

"I'll be sick,'' she mumbled, licking her lips. Leaving them shiny with moisture he wanted to taste.

Boyd stifled a groan. He really was a sorry so-and-so to be thinking erotic thoughts about tongues and lips meeting and mating when Stacy was so obviously suffering.

"Damn Jarrod,'' he muttered as he put aside the glass. But even as he cursed his friend, his mind put the lie to the words. Luke was a hell of a good doctor, as conscientious and cautious as any Boyd had ever known. Stacy had had all the expert attention and care that medical science could provide. What she needed now was rest.

"Easy, honey," he murmured, settling next to her on the couch with as much care as he could manage. The cushion dipped under his weight, nudging Stacy toward him. It seemed as natural as breathing to slip his arm behind her slender back and pull her even closer.

She murmured something he didn't catch before letting herself relax against him. Even with the added bulk of her pregnancy, she felt fragile in his arms. Like an angel he'd seen in one of the museums in New York Karen had dragged him through on their honeymoon. An angel with smudges under her eyes where the bruises were fading and life quickening in her belly.

Without intending to, he smoothed his hand over her hair before tugging it back from her face. Silky and cool, the soft strands caught in the tiny nicks of his fingertips before slipping away.

She stirred, then sighed and settled more firmly against him, like a child snuggling down for a nap. Or a woman offering her trust to a man she only barely knew.

He felt humbled and honored, emotions he'd felt only once before, when Karen had offered her heart and her innocence to him one rainy night an eternity ago.

He wasn't a man who put much store in answered prayers, or even second chances. A man was lucky if he loved once in a lifetime, even luckier if his love was returned. Twice wasn't in the cards. Not the hand he'd been dealt anyway.

Slowly, carefully, his big hand holding Stacy's silky head steady, he eased back to rest against the cushions. Beneath hers, his body felt acutely sensitive, his blood surging in rhythm with her breathing. Between them, the baby pressed snugly against his rib cage.

Boyd closed his eyes and breathed a prayer he wished rather than believed might be heard. *One more month. One lousy, short month is all I'm asking. Give the kid a chance, okay?*
*Please.*

# Eight

Stacy woke up to the inner pummeling of little fists, with a few hard kicks thrown in. Eyes still closed, she imagined Tory's tiny features screwed into an impatient frown and smiled.

"Good morning, sweet pea," she murmured, her voice still rusty from sleep.

"How are you feeling?" replied a deep voice.

Startled, she snapped open her eyes and shot a fast glance toward the sound. To her surprise, she discovered it wasn't morning at all, but evening, although she was too groggy to guess how long she'd been asleep. Not too groggy, however, to realize she was in a strange bed in a strange room that was in semidarkness, the only illumination coming from the hall beyond. Boyd was standing by an open closet door, a towel slung around his neck, watching her with intense gray eyes. He must have carried her into his bed, she realized—while she'd been completely oblivious.

She let out her breath slowly, far too conscious that he was wearing little more than a tattered pair of gray running shorts, slung precariously low on his hips where the elastic had stretched. Worn as thin and as slippery as silk, the soft-knitted cotton concealed little of his blatantly male form. Stacy felt her mouth go dry.

"I...must have fallen asleep," she said with a shaky smile.

"Out like a light." His mouth slanted. "I figured the meds you took put you down for the count, so I carried you in here to sleep it off. That sofa's pretty, but it's a bitch to sleep on."

She nodded and glanced around. In contrast to the lush living room, Boyd's bedroom was decidedly Spartan with white walls and simple furniture. The only color came from the books crammed into a floor-to-ceiling bookcase opposite and an exquisitely stitched quilt bunched at her feet.

"What time is it?" she asked when she realized he was watching her beneath drawn brows. She was beginning to get used to that tight little crease his frowns wedged above his nose whenever he was concentrating—or annoyed.

"Just past midnight."

He stepped closer, bringing the scents of a recent shower and shave with him. His hair was tousled and damp. Tendrils clung to his strong neck and curled against his forehead where the towel had left them. His chest was bare, save for the shimmering fan of sun-bleached hair. Like golden moss on a rock, it swirled around the tiny nipples before narrowing to a silky line that bisected his flat, corrugated midriff, then flared to encompass his navel where droplets of water shimmered like diamonds against his bronzed skin. Stacy felt her fingers pressing the sheet as a longing to swirl her fingers through that silken thatch swept through her.

"How's the head?" he asked, his voice thoughtfully muted.

"Still attached, but barely." She managed a laugh that proved to be a grave mistake when pain stabbed.

"Best not to move if you can help it." His bronzed face still wore a frown, and he looked tired and just a little harried. Guilt scurried into her mind and stayed as he pressed a broad, warm palm to her forehead. His touch was gentle, testing. His hand was rough, like velvet sandpaper, she thought, and wondered how those strong blunt fingers would feel against her ultrasensitive breasts.

"No fever," he said before withdrawing his hand. Her pulse, however, was rocketing.

"I'm fine, really," she murmured. A thread had raveled free at the hemline of his shorts, drawing her gaze to the perfect symmetry of strong, supple thigh muscles beneath the taut sun-burnished skin. A sprinkling of hair bleached nearly white curled like soft fuzz, tempting her to trace patterns against his flesh with her fingertips.

Her face warmed at the thought, and she took a breath to steady herself. Darn those rampaging hormones. If she wasn't careful, she'd be salivating soon.

Arcing her gaze upward, she found him studying her with hooded eyes. "Are you up to eating something?" he asked when their gazes met.

"I'm not hungry." Worse, her stomach was still queasy from the pills. "But hold that thought," she added after a moment's reflection. "By tomorrow morning I'll likely be hungry enough to eat this pillow."

One side of his mouth curled upward. "How about oatmeal instead?"

"Believe me, I'll never be that hungry." But she might be if she didn't find work soon, she admitted with a silent pang of raw panic.

"Maybe some tea?" he persisted. "I think I have some of the herbal stuff I keep around for Prudy in case she drops in to deliver one of her motherly lectures."

Stacy curved her lips into a smile at the thought of her diminutive friend laying down the law to a man twice her size. "All I really need right now is to sleep off the aftereffects of those blasted pills."

She felt a cramp threatening in one calf muscle and stretched out her leg, drawing his sudden gaze. Except for her shoes, she was lying fully clothed under the pale blue sheet, yet when he looked at her, she felt a blush climbing from a spot between her breasts to blanket her face. His expression didn't change, but suddenly she felt the crackle of electricity in the air. Like a sea change right before a storm, she thought.

"I didn't mean to wake you," he said, shifting his attention from her body to her face. "Karen always said I was more bull than cat, especially when I was trying to be quiet."

It was the first time he'd ever mentioned his wife to her, but she detected nothing more than a burr of self-mockery in his tone. "Don't apologize, please," she murmured, pushing to her elbows. "This is your house. Stomp around all you want. I promise I won't complain." Somehow she levered herself to a sitting position without too much huffing and puffing. "Tomorrow first thing, I'll start calling on apartments for rent."

He shifted, his hands wrapping around the ends of the towel still slung around his neck. When he moved, his muscles bunched and flexed in a dance of tightly wrapped power that fascinated her. Len had been a strong man, but Boyd's body was a magnificent sculpture of grace and controlled force.

"Don't take this wrong, but when I stopped by your place this afternoon, your landlord told me you hadn't been able to make the rent."

Wattchel, you bigmouthed bastard, Stacy thought, grinding her teeth. Then, realizing that Boyd was watching her, forced herself to relax. "I admit I came up a little short this month." She shrugged. "The usual post-divorce regrouping. Friends who've been through it assure me this too shall pass."

"Any idea when?"

Stacy glanced at the firm set to his jaw. Leave it to him to cut straight to the question she'd asked every day since the accident. "Actually, I've been toying with the idea of asking a psychic."

He offered her a sardonic look. "Look, if it would help—"

"You've already helped," she hastened to assure him. Since Len's illness, she had lost a great deal that mattered to her. Pride was one of the few things she had managed to salvage.

"Stacy, I'm not offering charity. Just a loan."

"And I'm declining your offer." She drew breath. "With thanks."

"Damn it, Stacy, I'm…I was a doctor. I know what damage the kind of trauma you suffered can do. Only a few hours ago, you damn near passed out from pain. Right now you've got about much color in your face as the wall behind you.''

Stacy drew a breath. His anger was palpable. She refused to accept that it was justified. ''I admit I'm a little shaky, but that's because of the pills. By tomorrow morning I'll—''

''Tomorrow morning you'll still only be three days out of the hospital. Most patients with your history take a good month to regain even a decent amount of strength.'' Boyd raked an impatient hand through his hair, leaving it even more tousled. ''Jarrod never should have discharged you.''

Stacy felt herself coloring. She considered lying, but her gratitude to Dr. Jarrod wouldn't allow her to let him take the blame. ''It wasn't his fault. I...asked to leave.'' She steeled herself to meet Boyd's accusing gaze. ''My bill was already so high.'' Even with liberal repayment terms, she'd be sending the hospital a check once a month for years—and she'd yet to find a job.

He muttered an obscenity that made her wince. ''So bottom line, in order to save money, you're willing to risk your baby's life.''

She gasped. ''No, of course not! I love Tory.''

He narrowed his gaze, searing her. ''Sure you do, but hey, you have your pride, right? Maybe you don't have a place to live or food to eat or even a blanket for the baby, but by God, you've held on to those almighty principles of yours.'' He offered a grunt of disgust. ''Way I see it, I figure the odds at ten to one against your carrying that baby more than two weeks longer. And I'm being generous.''

Stacy stared at him, unable to speak as tears welled in her eyes. ''Don't say that,'' she whispered brokenly. ''D-don't even *believe* that.''

Boyd felt a hand squeeze his heart. He hadn't intended to come on so strong. But somehow, once he started, he couldn't seem to stop. Sickened by the things he'd said to her yet unable to take back the words, he walked to the window and drew back the curtains.

As a kid, he'd loved to sit on the roof outside his attic room and watch the stars. He tried to count them once, but there had been too many. All those wishes just waiting to be granted, his grandmother used to say. If there were stars up there now, he couldn't see them.

"Karen wanted to stay another night at the coast," he said, staring out into the murky darkness beyond the streetlight. "She was crazy about the ocean. But I said no, we couldn't afford another night. What I meant was *I* couldn't afford it. She offered to pay from her own account. I said no." Remembering that last bitter argument, he let his voice trail off until he'd sorted through all the things he could say. Should say.

"And then she'd cried," he said, feeling his way. "I compromised and said we could stay the day, drive home that night." He felt his throat close up and took a breath. "It was foggy and cold, a lousy time to be driving narrow roads. I remember reminding myself to watch out for deer, and the next thing I remember headlights were coming right for us, and Karen was screaming."

Stacy heard Boyd's voice change and bit her lip. She wanted to tell him to stop torturing himself, that he didn't have to go on. But some sixth sense kept her silent. Perhaps, by listening while he purged himself of black memory she could repay him in some small measure for all he'd done for her.

"We'd gone off the road, down into this gully. It was like some kind of weird carnival ride, only in slow motion. A thicket of blackberry bushes stopped us at the bottom." He fell silent, swamped by memories of a fog-enshrouded nightmare—struggling to push his way out of the car, thrashing his way through the tangle of thorns and cane in order to extricate Karen from the passenger side. She'd been dazed. In shock. Her eyes accusing him in the light reflected by the car's headlights.

"God, it was cold," he remembered aloud. "Karen kept apologizing because she couldn't make her teeth stop chattering." He'd wrapped her in his jacket and tied his sweatshirt around her neck, but nothing had stopped the violent shudders racking her body. *The baby,* she'd cried, digging frantic fingers into his shoulder even as he lifted her into his arms. Somehow he'd staggered up the incline, praying with every step that someone would come along to help. A trucker, a tourist, a local resident returning to a house tucked into a wrinkle in the wild landscape. Someone. Anyone.

But there had been no one. Nothing but an icy fog and a road stretching into darkness. They told him later that he'd walked five miles with Karen in his arms. Endless, cold miles. Taking a breath, he willed steel into his voice. There wasn't much to tell. "The contractions started before she got to the hospital. She...never lost consciousness. Luke did everything he could, but it was too soon."

Stacy realized she was holding her breath and rationed it out slowly, afraid to make even the slightest sound. For reasons of his own, Boyd had opened up to her, telling her things she suspected he'd never told anyone else. A lump formed in her throat when she realized he was offering her something she sensed he rarely gave—his trust.

"If we'd been closer to the hospital, if Karen had gotten immediate help..." He shrugged and turned to face her. His face was impassive, his eyes darkened nearly to black and heartbreakingly remote. Stacy clamped down hard on her lower lip in order to keep from crying out.

"The official cause of death was internal injuries caused by the accident, but I know better." His words were close to lifeless now, as though he'd shut himself off from everything but the need to finish his story. "Karen died because I couldn't swallow my damned pride and let her pay for another night at the coast. A lousy eighty dollars, Stacy. That's all it would have cost. I make more than that in a couple of hours now, for all the good it does me."

He closed his eyes, his throat working as he battled emotions she suspected he had kept hidden for a long time. "I wake up every morning knowing that I killed my wife and child," he said when he had himself under control again. "I don't want you to have to live every day in that same hell."

"Boyd, it wasn't—"

He cut her off, his voice rasping over each word. "I'm offering you a place to stay until you're strong enough to handle things on your own. And a job if you want it—helping me sort through months of paperwork I've been putting off. Nine dollars an hour, the going rate for temporary clerical help, last time I checked.''

Eyes bleak, jaw hard, he strode past the end of the bed to the walk-in closet and disappeared inside without giving her a chance to respond. Seconds later, he returned, his long legs sheathed in jeans, a cotton work shirt hanging open over his chest. He had his shoes in one hand, the blue towel in the other. A twist of his wrist sent the towel looping over a chair across the room.

''Where are you going?'' Stacy cried, her voice shaking.

Boyd saw the fatigue under the tears glistening on her white cheeks and felt like a heel. Worse.

''You need rest, and I need to walk off some steam.''

He yanked open a drawer, pulled out a pair of socks and sat down on the chair to pull them on. Each movement he made was controlled, his lean body radiating tension. Stacy could only guess at the anguish it had cost him to break open old wounds.

After freeing herself from the covers, she went to him just as he got to his feet. ''I'm sorry about Karen and the baby,'' she murmured. ''But you have to know it wasn't your fault.''

''Yes,'' he said quietly, firmly. ''It was.'' He would have walked around her, but Stacy caught his arm, halting him. His gaze was remote, his face stony, as though he were already having second thoughts about opening the door to his past even a little.

''I... '' She stopped, let out an unsteady breath. There was no sense arguing with him. Not about his mistaken feelings of guilt. Not about her mistaken pride. He was right. She'd been foolish to insist that Dr. Jarrod release her. Foolish and selfish.

''I'm scared, Boyd,'' she admitted, her voice trembling and thin. ''Scared that you might be right. That I might lose my baby, too. I know I should have stayed in the hospital, but...'' Her lips trembled, and her eyes filled. ''I swore I was through crying.''

Without a word he gathered her close, one big hand guiding her head to his shoulder. She closed her eyes and held on, her fingers digging into his back. He was warm and solid, a bulwark against the terrible fear.

"It's okay, honey," he murmured, his breath warm against her temple. "Go ahead and bawl your eyes out if you want. Might even do you some good."

She swallowed, tasted tears. "No, it's not good for Tory. I read that babies are as sensitive to their mom's mood as they are to physical stimuli."

"Then maybe we should see about changing yours." Boyd tilted her head up, his hand warm on her cheek. She let her eyes drift open and found him watching her. His eyes were dark. Kind. She started to thank him, only to have his mouth brush hers.

"Let me take care of you," he whispered gruffly. "Take care of both of you, until you're strong enough to handle things on your own." His mouth brushed hers again. Softly. Gently.

She tasted compassion, felt long-buried desires stir inside her. It seemed like forever that her world had been bounded by Len's madness on one side and the demands she'd made on herself to remain strong for the baby's sake and her own. It felt so good to be held in arms that were stronger than hers, if only for a few minutes out of a truly lousy day.

Boyd felt her melt against him and schooled himself to maintain a careful distance, even as he sensed something slipping deep inside himself. She was vulnerable and afraid. Still in a kind of emotional shock. She needed comfort and support, not a sexual come-on from a horny bastard who'd just spent twenty minutes lecturing himself under an icy shower about honor and decency.

He'd been damn near blue from hypothermia by the time he'd gotten his unruly libido tamed. As long as Stacy was under his roof, she was off-limits. No matter how warm and giving her body felt against his. No matter how sweet her lips might taste.

It didn't matter that he couldn't seem to breathe properly when she was in the same room, or that she had only to look at him with those golden eyes for him to want her. She was still recovering from trauma and she had nearly lost her baby. If she let him help, he intended to watch over her like a damn mother cat. Even if he felt more like a mangy tom on the prowl.

Fighting a need that just skirted the edge of savage, he rested his cheek against her hair and stroked her back with fingers that weren't as steady as he wished.

"Feeling better?" he asked when he was sure he had control of his voice.

Smiling, bemused, she drew back, her stomach still nestling lightly against his corded belly. Hesitantly she brought her hand to his face, her fingers skimming the hard planes, the pleasantly rough beard.

"Oh, Boyd, how can I ever thank you enough?" she whispered. "What would I have done without you these last few days?"

"You've thanked me enough for two lifetimes, so cut it out, hear?"

"But—"

"Trust me, Stacy. I need you more than you need me."

She doubted that very much and said so.

His eyes crinkled at the corners. "You haven't seen the mess on my desk," he said, arcing backward just enough to bring them eye to eye. And thigh to thigh, hard contours of muscle against soft flesh. Her mind made a quick detour into thoughts of opening her thighs to him, and she felt her face warming. An estrogen rush, she reminded herself. Mother Nature's way of prodding an expectant female to bond with a protective male. Evidently her body considered Boyd MacAuley a prime candidate.

"Maybe I should hold out for a higher wage." She attempted to ease backward, out of his embrace, but his arms refused to yield.

"Take it or leave it, Ms. Patterson." Laughter rumbled beneath the stern tone of his voice, and she felt the corners of her mouth lifting. Right now, this instant, she felt young again. Able to leap tall buildings with a single bound and catch bullets in her teeth. When she was in Boyd's arms, the future didn't seem quite so grim.

"I guess I'll take it." She drew a quick breath before adding, "But only if we get one thing straight. I'm not sleeping in your bed."

Frowning, he cut a glance toward the rumpled sheets. "If you're worried about some kind of sleazy proposition, forget it." This time he was the one who stepped back, and she felt chilled by the absence of his body heat.

"That wasn't what I meant at all," she assured him. Her headache was coming back, and she was feeling strangely detached from her body. "I know that you...that I...what I *meant* to say was that I'll only stay if I'm not putting you out." She frowned. "Of your bed."

"Does that mean you're inviting me to share?"

"No, of course not."

"Even if I promise not to hog the covers or tickle your feet?" His tone was teasing, his eyes nearly smiling. He was so close she could see that his thick eyelashes were tipped in gold and that his gray eyes were shot through with jagged shards of sea green.

She took a breath and started over. "I mean, I'm sure I'll be perfectly comfortable on the sofa," she said firmly.

He shook his head. "Too narrow for the two of you. Most likely end up on the floor before the night is over."

He shifted his gaze to her belly. Perversely, or perhaps because the baby agreed with him, Tory gave a hard kick. Stacy winced, then sighed and lifted a hand to massage the now-tender spot on her abdomen. "Okay, I get the message."

"Gave you a kick, did she?"

Stacy smiled. "A good one. I'm beginning to think she just might end up to be the first female placekicker in the history of the NFL." She felt another kick and laughed softly. "She's also, I'm sorry to say, a definite night person. Tends to sleep all day and then wants to party all night. I've spoken severely to her several times, but she doesn't pay the least bit of attention."

"Sounds like a challenge." His voice had a hollow quality,

as though he were still trapped somewhere between the present and the nightmare past he'd just revisited. Hadn't Prudy told her that the child he'd lost had been a little girl?

"Would...would you like to feel for yourself?" she blurted. Before he could answer, she took his hand and pressed it to the spot where Tory's tiny foot still rested. Little imp that she was, Tory responded to the slight pressure by giving another healthy kick, squarely in the middle of Boyd's broad palm.

A look of terrible sadness passed over his face. He closed his eyes for an instant and bowed his head. And then his face changed. Hardened. Even before he stepped back and let his arms fall to his sides, she realized she'd crossed some kind of line. Like walking from the warmth of a summer day into a frigid, barren room.

"Boyd, I'm sorry," she murmured quickly, before he could turn away. "I should have realized—"

"It's late. You need sleep, and I need a drink." A heartbeat later, he'd grabbed his keys and wallet from the dresser and was on his way out.

Away from his own house.

Away from her and her bungling attempts to comfort him.

Stacy woke up at 4:00 a.m. on the dot. For the past month, ever since Tory had started taking up most of the room in her mama's abdomen, Stacy hadn't been able to go more than three hours between visits to the bathroom. One of the lesser joys of pregnancy, she reminded herself peevishly as she padded into the hall. The bathroom was the first door to her right. Farther along the short hall another door was firmly closed.

Boyd's office? she wondered as she slipped into the john and shut the door behind her. A few minutes later she retraced her steps, still blinking from the glare of the bathroom light.

She was about to slip back into bed when she heard a guttural cry coming from the direction of the living room, followed by the low rumble of Boyd's voice, rasping out strident snatches of words. Curses. Bits of unconnected sentences. Nothing that made sense except to tell her he was suffering. Battling demons from his past he'd unleashed in an effort to help her, she suspected. Shivering in the sudden chill, she rounded the bed and hurried toward the sound.

The living room was shrouded in darkness, relieved only by the faint glow from the streetlighting shining through the front window. Hand extended, she picked her way through a maze of dark shapes and lighter upholstery, heading toward the sofa where Boyd was lying on his back, one arm resting on his chest, the other dangling to the floor. Once again he'd stripped to the running shorts, which had slipped below his navel.

She was a few feet away when she stumbled over something. Glancing down, she saw a jumble of sofa cushions, the ones forming the cushy backrest she'd appreciated earlier tossed aside, she assumed, to make room for his large body. Clearly, from the look of his awkward position, not enough room.

Her heart went out to him and thudded a few heavy beats before she hauled it back. Boyd MacAuley not only didn't want her sympathy; he would damn sure throw it back in her face if she so much as tried to sneak it past that stiff guard of his.

That decided, she bent closer and murmured his name. When he didn't respond, she called louder, straining to force a lilt into her voice. He muttered something, protesting, then cried out. At the same time he opened his eyes, as though the sound of his own voice had jerked him from the tumble of bad dreams.

"What's wrong?" he said, uncoiling instantly to loom above her. "Are you in pain again?"

Stacy couldn't remember ever being so touched before. Here he was, his eyes still dark and tormented from the nightmare she'd interrupted, worried that she was in trouble. It took her a couple of swallows before she trusted her voice not to betray her feelings.

"Actually, I, um, was having trouble sleeping and thought some of that herbal tea you mentioned might do the trick."

He swiped a hand through his hair and stared at her.

"Tea?"

She nodded. "I apologize for waking you, but I didn't want to be banging pans around in your kitchen without your permission."

He glanced toward the kitchen, then back at her face. She managed a smile, which slipped a little when he clamped two large hands on her shoulders. "I'll get it. You head on back to bed where it's warm."

Warm? It had to be close to eighty, even with the windows open. She was about to protest when she noticed the hard set of his jaw. Pick your battles, her crusading journalist father had always counseled. And since her goal had been to extricate Boyd from the nightmare images plaguing him, she silently let him turn her toward the bedroom.

"Scoot," he ordered gruffly, as though she were four years old and making a nuisance of herself. Which, she decided was exactly what she was doing. But at least the black despair that had been in his eyes when he'd opened them was gone. It wasn't much of a gift to give him, but, at the moment, it was all she had, so it would have to do.

"Two sugars," she called over her shoulder as she padded toward his bedroom and a nest of pale blue sheets that smelled like the man who usually slept there. If she had to drink herbal tea, which she'd always hated, at least it would be sweet.

# Nine

$S$tacy was having a lovely dream of a springtime picnic and a man's hard body pressing hers to soft, sweet grass when she was jolted awake by a muffled thud, followed by a terse masculine curse.

Boyd's wife had been right. He was built more for strength than grace, but as he edged out of the closet with his heavy work boots in one hand, a worn leather belt in the other and a khaki work shirt slung over his shoulder, he was trying his best to be quiet.

Obviously in the middle of dressing for work, he was wearing an old-fashioned ribbed undershirt that clung to his corded belly like a second skin before stretching thin over the heavy muscles of his chest. As always, he was wearing jeans, all but one of the metal buttons undone.

Seeing that she was awake, he scowled, creasing his forehead into well-worn grooves. "Sorry," he muttered. "Damn boot just slipped."

Smiling, she lay still, her dream still lingering like the scent of spring flowers, its sunshine filling the bedroom. "Not a problem," she slurred, rubbing her cheek against the pillow.

Her dream had been sex and skin and sunshine, and his big hands had been caressing the swollen contours of her belly, his fingers sure and steady and his eyes dark with desire instead of the hard-edged worry she was beginning to associate with him. With a heavy sigh, she forced her eyes to sharper focus.

"At least I got the sunshine right," she muttered, reluctant to let go of the delicious sensations she'd been experiencing only a few oblivious moments earlier. With a sigh, she pushed her hair away from her face then went about the cumbersome task of sitting up. Never again would she take a waistline for granted, she decided, stifling a yawn. For as long as she could remember, she'd had a tendency to dawdle in the twilight warmth between sleep and waking for as long as possible before reluctantly rousing herself to full consciousness. Since her accident, however, and the concussion, she'd had even more trouble.

"I figured you'd need some things from the market so I'll swing by around noon and take you shopping." Boyd dropped his boots by the chair before shrugging into his shirt.

"I'll be fine, really."

Boyd buttoned a couple of buttons before shoving his shirt-tails into the jeans. "You'll need milk and fresh vegetables," he continued as though she hadn't spoken. "Juice."

"Boyd, don't fuss."

He spared her an impatient look before threading his belt through the loops with those clever hands she'd dreamed of feeling on her breasts. "Last I heard, Prudy was working days so she won't be around, and there's no phone where I'm working, so if you need...anything, call 911. Got that?"

Stacy had an urge to snap off a salute, but made herself nod solemnly instead. "Got it."

"Promise?"

"I promise."

Boyd heard a subtle note of amused exasperation in her tone and made himself back off, even as he mentally added the purchase of a cellular phone to his shopping list. Jaw tight, he cinched his belt and shoved his feet into his boots, conscious that Stacy had drawn her knees to her belly and was resting her chin on them, watching him with that mixture of curiosity and admiration that had his blood surging every time he was within shouting distance.

It was bad enough that he'd sweated, sworn and paced his way through the rest of a sleepless night, trying to figure ways to help her without smashing himself bloody against that blasted pride of hers. By sunup, he'd chewed his way through enough stupid ideas to give himself a giant bellyache. Long about the time he'd hauled himself into the kitchen to make coffee, he'd suddenly remembered he hadn't thought to grab clean clothes when he'd delivered her 4:00 a.m. tea. Which meant that unless he intended to face the owners of the Victorian in a wrinkled shirt smelling of sweat and spilled beer from his halfhearted binge of the night before, he would have to sneak into his own bedroom for another one.

He'd told himself it was no big deal. Hell, he'd seen women sleeping before. Too many times to count, in fact. Young, old. Beautiful, plain. Oblivious to his presence. Patients, a handful of lovers in the years before he'd met Karen. Even Prudy, who had a tendency to fall asleep in midsentence after a particularly hard grind in the ER.

Stacy was different. Special. She'd lost her husband to a madness that would have destroyed her, too, if she hadn't had the guts to walk away. Lost him again in a split second of grinding metal. And yet, she'd been able to come back, if not completely whole, close enough to face another set of problems. Like an empty wallet, no place to live and a baby on the way. And still, she teased and laughed and generally lit up his house in a way that scared him to the bone.

Damn, but he admired her. More than anything, he wanted to keep her safe from the kind of sadness he knew was waiting if she lost that baby she loved so much. Once made, he was determined to act on that decision.

His body, however, was determined to act on another. The one that had his blood steaming and his hunger simmering.

Watching her as she'd slept had honed the blunted edges of his control until his need for her was sharp enough to slice steel. His conscience was already clawing at him for a long list of sins stretching back to the age of five when he took his first pull on his old man's whiskey bottle. But this latest one was pitiful, even for him.

But damn, he wanted her. Hot and sweet, buried to the hilt inside her. Pouring out his loneliness and grief and pain in one violent rush. His body ached with it, even as he told himself he deserved to burn in the worst fires of hell.

Even now, in the bright light of day with her eyes still filled with weariness and her face far too pale, he wanted to slip beneath the sheet covering her and pull her close.

He felt his body stir and knew he was only a whisper away from doing just that. Scowling, he shot to his feet and headed for the door.

"I made tea," he all but growled over his shoulder. "I'll get you a cup before I head out."

Boyd tossed aside the ancient issue of *National Geographic* without finishing the article on a newly discovered Inca burial site he'd been grimly plowing through for the past ten minutes, and checked his watch one more time.

It was still early, not yet eight. So far, he was the only one in the small waiting room adjacent to PortGen's birthing suites. He was there to see Luke Jarrod.

A man of careful habits like himself, Luke always started rounds at six unless he happened to be attending a birth. Damn the luck, Boyd thought sourly, eyeing the bright orange double doors directly in front of him.

They'd been blue the last time he'd been in this part of the hospital. The last time he'd been there, of course, was after Karen's accident. He tried to stop the memories, but they came back on a rush. By the time the ambulance had gotten Karen to the delivery room and she'd been prepped, the baby's head had been crowning. Tiny enough to cradle in his hand, she'd been perfectly formed, with downy blond fuzz for hair and a quizzical look that broke his heart. He'd nearly burst with pride when she'd opened her eyes and struggled to focus her milky blue gaze on her daddy's face. Every night for months he'd seen those eyes whenever he'd closed his own.

Anna Elena MacAuley had lived less than ten minutes. Not even technology's latest and best could compensate for lungs that hadn't had time to fully develop. Karen had been too weak to cry for her baby. He'd been too angry. Ten minutes later he'd lost Karen, too.

He remembered Luke's anguished curses, the stunned faces of the nurses, the hushed voices, the sideways glances of pity. Someone—Luke, he thought—had led him to an empty room and moments later, shoved a cup of scalding coffee into his hands.

What he'd said, when he'd left the hospital was a blank. He knew he'd walked for a long time in the clammy chill of a winter fog, walked until he couldn't walk any farther. He'd gotten home somehow, and he'd slept like the dead for eighteen hours.

The hospital had offered him a month's leave. Time to grieve, the chief of surgery had explained with an awkward kindness he'd never forgotten. He'd taken two weeks, then gone back to work, too restless to relax. Too wired to rest. After a period of walking on eggs, his peers had gradually relaxed and the days had fallen into a familiar routine. No one talked about Karen or the baby, for which he was grateful.

A month passed. Two. Winter bled into spring. Daffodils bloomed. He painted his house and learned to cook after his own fashion. That year at Easter weekend, the mercury dipped and the expected rain turned to sleet. Accident victims started arriving early and by evening, every OR had a waiting list. By midnight plasma and whole blood was in short supply, and they'd gone through countless boxes of surgical gloves by the time he'd finished prepping for yet one more procedure.

The patient was young and female and in bad shape with a ruptured spleen and related trauma. He'd had her belly open and the bleeders clamped and was about to excise the torn spleen when, for no reason he'd ever been able to identify, he'd glanced at her face—and seen Karen.

Weeks later they'd told him that he'd finished the operation, stripped off his gloves and disappeared. When he hadn't shown up for his shift the next day, they'd called Prudy on her day off to check on him. She'd found him sitting in a rocking chair in the baby's nursery, still in his scrubs, holding the teddy bear he'd bought months earlier.

The damn bear was still in the nursery, crumpled in a corner of the crib where he'd thrown it in a towering rage. He had himself under control now. For long stretches of time he actually managed to forget he'd snapped. And then, for no reason at all, his vision would blur and his hands would begin to tremble.

So far he'd always been alone, and he intended to keep it that way, which was one of the reasons he'd avoided PortGen and the people who'd known him then. Everyone but Prudy, and that was because he couldn't very well avoid his next-door neighbor.

Needing to move, he got to his feet and walked to the elevator alcove for a drink of water from the fountain there. He heard the distant ringing of a phone, the swish of automatic doors. Hushed voices.

His heart thudded and a hole opened in his belly. He felt a wild need to escape. Gritting his teeth, he retraced his steps and took a seat where he'd be sure to see Luke on his way through.

It was nearly quarter past eight by the time the doors swished open and Luke came loping through. Older than Boyd by six or seven years, he was still lean and fit and had routinely worn Boyd to a nub on the racquetball court. Catching sight of Boyd, he stopped in midstride, his mouth going slack for beat before breaking into a grin. His thick black hair was shot with silver but the deep-set eyes Karen had once called Paul Newman blue were as sharply assessing as ever.

"MacAuley, you sonofagun." He came forward to pump Boyd's hand. "It's damn good to see you, son. Damn good."

"Good enough to bend a few rules?"

Luke narrowed his gaze. "Depends on the rules and the reasons."

Boyd drew a breath. He'd never been good at asking for favors or anything else. "Stacy Patterson. I'd like your read on her prognosis."

"Sure, no problem."

The doors swished open again, drawing Boyd's gaze to a burly orderly pushing a woman on a gurney. From the look of elation on her face and on the face of the man walking next to her, holding her hand, she had just had a baby.

"One of yours?" he asked when he caught Luke studying him.

"Yep. Third one since yesterday morning. All girls."

Boyd managed a polite nod. "Any...problems?"

"Nary a one, thank the good Lord." Luke flexed his shoulders, then glanced toward the coffee machine at the end of the corridor. "You got any quarters on you?"

Frowning, Boyd dug into his pocket and pulled out a handful of change. "Enough for two cups of that poison," he said after he'd sorted through the coins.

"So you've fallen for one of my patients, heh?" Luke drawled as he watched Boyd plugging the machine.

Boyd shot his friend a look that had Luke lifting both hands in surrender. "My mistake," he drawled. "Wishful thinking, most likely."

"Shot in the dark, you mean." Boyd handed Luke a cup filled with murky black liquid exuding a pungent aroma of burnt beans along with the steam. Luke nodded his thanks before taking a sip.

"Stuff tastes like engine sludge," he muttered as Boyd retrieved his own cup from the machine's window. "Ruins a man for good coffee, sure enough."

As though by some prearranged agreement, the two men walked toward the door leading to a small patio tucked into a concrete canyon formed by the mental health wing on one side and a retaining wall on the other. Twin metal tables and a clutch of mismatched chairs sat under faded umbrellas, one of which had taken on a precarious list to one side. What sunshine managed to spill over the hospital's tall roof was watery and pale.

"How's Marlyssa these days?" Boyd asked as he settled into the nearest chair.

Luke grimaced as he eased into the chair opposite. "Last I heard she was married to a CPA and deliriously happy spending the poor guy's money."

"Should I say I'm sorry?"

Luke shrugged before leaning back. "I wanted kids. She didn't."

Marlyssa Evans had gone to the same fancy private school with Karen and had been a bridesmaid at their wedding where Luke had taken one look at the raven-haired debutante and pounced. The sexual energy between them had been enough to light the city, and though the hospital odds makers had given their affair a week, it had lasted a good four or five years. Longer than Boyd's marriage, in fact.

"So, what's the deal with you and Mrs. Patterson?" Luke asked after the silence between them turned awkward.

Boyd hooked an empty chair closer and propped his foot on the seat. "No deal. I'm just looking after her until she can pull things together on her own."

Luke studied the contents of his cup, his expression grave. "Did she tell you she'd been released against medical advice?"

"Yeah, she told me. I take it you weren't pleased?'

Luke snorted before downing another mouthful. "We went toe to toe for damn near an hour. I pulled out all the stops. Gave a great lecture on the unpredictable aftereffects of concussion. Warned her that prolonged stress can cause fetal instability." He shook his head, then sighed. "The woman is as adorable as a week-old kitten, and as stubborn as any jenny I've ever had the sorry misfortune to meet."

"She's broke. Busted. 'Post-divorce regrouping,' she called it." Boyd scowled. He could still see the lumpy sofa bed in her dingy apartment and the secondhand dresser she'd fixed up for the baby. Now even those things were gone, sold off by Wattchel, along with just about everything else.

"So that's what this is all about—my fee." Luke chuckled.

"Hell, Boyd, you didn't have to spring for coffee to convince me to write it off."

"No can do. She'd know it was charity." He glanced up to find the other man studying him with a thoughtful glint in his blue eyes.

"You have a better idea?"

"Charge her enough to make it seem realistic, then send me a bill for the rest of it." Boyd lifted his cup to his mouth and slugged down the bitter liquid. It burned his gullet and soured his stomach, but he needed the caffeine. "And take your time while you're at it."

"You got it. Anything else?"

Boyd felt his gut tighten. "No bull, Luke. What are her chances of having a normal delivery?"

"If she follows doctor's orders to avoid stress, long trips by car, and lifting anything heavier than a book, excellent. In another couple of weeks or so, if there are no further complications, she'll be able to resume normal activities in moderation."

"Care to be more specific?"

"Short trips by car, light housework, moderate exercise, a sedentary job," Luke said slowly. "Slow and easy sex with a considerate partner—in case you're interested."

Boyd scowled. "Get stuffed, Jarrod."

"Might be the best thing the doctor could prescribe. For both of you."

Boyd shifted, his shoulders suddenly tight. He'd asked all the questions he'd come to ask but one. Sitting straighter, he drew a breath. "What about the baby?"

"Far as I can tell, as healthy as they come. Amnio came back clean, and the fetal heartbeat's strong. Looks like the kid's a survivor like her mom." Luke's voice carried a quiet confidence Boyd had learned to trust, and he felt the tension coiled like a snake in his belly ease off.

"One more question. Why did you want her to stay for a few more days?"

"A precaution, mostly." Luke drained his cup before crushing it in one hand to a lumpy ball. "At least that's what I put on the chart."

"What the hell does that mean?"

Luke grinned. "Maybe you haven't noticed, old son, but that is one good-looking, sexy lady."

"Maybe *you* haven't noticed, *old son*, but she's also your patient."

Luke's grin took on wolf edges. "Yeah, some guys have all the luck."

Boyd had the feeling Luke was jerking his chain and gave some thought to erasing that damned predatory grin with a right cross. "She's also pregnant."

"Granted. Otherwise, she wouldn't *be* my patient."

"Which means she's off-limits, you horny bastard."

"Sad to say, you're right—about both." Luke sighed, then lifted his face to the sun. "For what it's worth, if she *weren't* my patient, I'd be polishing my courtin' skills right quick."

"The hell you would!"

Luke stretched out his long legs and closed his eyes. "You being half-dead these days, you probably didn't notice how pretty she is under those bruises. Has soft skin, too. Real touchable like." He opened one eye and sighted on Boyd's face before closing it again. "Seems to me a man would consider himself blessed to taste a mouth like hers more than once in a lifetime, but then, you already know that, you lucky bastard." He sighed and opened his eyes. "Guess you forgot how it is in a hospital, son. Ain't no such thing as privacy."

Boyd felt his stomach muscles twisting into angry knots and muttered a curse that won him a chuckle.

"Last I heard Schultz had started a pool on the exact date and time of the wedding."

Boyd got to his feet, his expression as controlled as his temper. "Take my advice. Don't waste your money." He tossed his cup into a nearby trash receptacle and was about to leave when the door opened and Prudy entered the patio.

"Is this a private party or can anyone play?" she chirped as she approached, a cup of coffee in one hand, a paper plate containing a donut wrapped in cellophane in the other. She was wearing a smock of neon pink splotched with purple over white uniform trousers and green sneakers. In spite of the bright array, Boyd decided she looked tired.

"Mornin', gorgeous," Luke drawled, sitting up straighter. "Sit yourself down and take a load off."

"Are you coming or going?" she asked Boyd when she reached the table.

"Going."

Prudy heard the rasp of irritation in Boyd's tone and wondered what Luke could have said to put it there. "In that case, have a nice day and don't fall off any ladders."

That earned her a look meant to warn her off and she smiled to herself as she set her coffee and donut on the table. In the past week she'd seen more life in Boyd MacAuley than she or anyone else, she suspected, had seen since he'd cleaned out his locker in the doctors' lounge.

"He's got it bad," she muttered as Boyd disappeared into the building. "Has all the signs of a man on the brink of falling in love and fighting it with everything he has."

Luke nodded, his eyes crinkling at the corners. "I figure it's terminal."

Laughing, she settled herself in the chair Boyd had just vacated. "Unless I've totally lost my diagnostic skills, the lady in question is crazy for the guy."

"You think he's over Karen yet?"

Considering, Prudy concentrated on unwrapping the lemon-filled pastry. Boyd and Stacy were so utterly perfect for each other—empathetic, caring people who'd been hurt.

"Remember how terrible he looked at the funeral?" she asked slowly, seeing Boyd's too-pale features, the look of a half-crazed animal in his eyes.

Luke nodded, his blue eyes suddenly bleak as though he, too, were reliving that day. "Don't get your hopes up for a happy ending, Prue, cause I got me a feelin' it just ain't gonna happen."

# Ten

A gourmet meal it wasn't, Stacy decided as she added a sprinkle of shredded cheddar cheese to the salad she'd concocted from wilted lettuce, a handful of pecans and a couple of hard-boiled eggs. For the dressing she'd mixed mayonnaise and ketchup, coming up with a decent Thousand Island clone.

Wiping her hands on a spotless towel she'd found stashed in one of the cabinet drawers, she frowned down at the haphazard lunch—frozen pizza, a makeshift salad and, for dessert, peanut butter cups from the bag she'd found in Boyd's sadly depleted larder.

As for the kitchen, it was a cook's dream, with every sort of appliance. It was also darn near surgically sterile, without even a crumb to mar the pristine perfection of the silverware drawer. Unlike her own place—when she'd had one—where she tended to leave things where she'd last used them, his house was organized with a brutally logical precision. Everywhere but the room at the end of the hall.

Biting her lip, she treated the already spotless counter to another quick wipe with a damp dishcloth, her mind going again to the sight that had greeted her earlier this morning when she'd opened the door to what she'd thought was Boyd's office and discovered the wreckage of what had once been a charming nursery.

Stunned and dismayed, she could only imagine the depth of Boyd's grief as he'd torn the room apart. Destroying a crib and rocking chair until they were no more than sticks of white-painted kindling. Smashing lamps and figurines until nothing was left but brightly colored shards littering the off-white carpet like obscene confetti after a drunken brawl. In her mind she saw him using those large hands to tear apart stuffed tigers and bears and penguins once meant to win smiles from a much-loved baby girl.

Stacy couldn't prevent herself from shuddering again, just as she'd shuddered when she'd first seen the carnage. Boyd had faced his own kind of madness, she realized. And survived—after a fashion.

Now he repaired houses instead of bodies. A man who cried out in his sleep and hated himself for being alive. A man who'd taken her into his arms with a tenderness that still brought tears to her eyes, and kissed her with lonely hunger he was determined to deny.

A flash of color caught her eye, and she turned back to see Boyd coming up the walk, carrying a large cardboard box, his long legs eating the distance with an ease she, with her present waddling gait, envied.

There was something wonderfully earthy about a man in torn thigh-hugging jeans and a tight T-shirt stained in a jagged vee at the neck by the sweat of his labor, she decided, her heart suddenly taking off on a ragged gallop—something primitive and powerfully male that few women could resist. At least she couldn't, she realized, inhaling deeply.

"Hi," she said with decent enough composure as he stepped inside. "You're just in time for lunch."

He bunched his eyebrows into that intimidating crease she was beginning to anticipate and shot a fast glance around the kitchen. "I figured we'd go out."

She suspected he ate out a lot. Alone in a crowd of people.

"I didn't know how much time you could spare so I just improvised." She waved a hand toward the table where she'd laid out plates and silverware. And linen napkins she'd found in a drawer above the towels.

"Everything's ready, except for the pizza. According to the label, it'll take eighteen minutes. In case you want to wash up, or whatever."

While Stacy busied herself putting the pizza in the oven, Boyd set the box on the floor next to the fridge and took his time straightening. He'd been surprised to find her waiting for him in the kitchen, wearing a smile as soft and shy as a virgin's. Surprised and shaken by the surge of emotion that had filled him at the sight of her. He held his breath for a moment, trying to calm the violent rush of his blood. It was impossible.

All morning long he'd thought about her as he'd worked. Worried about her. Tried not to think about her curled up in his bed, nuzzling his pillow with her soft cheek. Tried not to want her so much his skin burned at the thought of touching her again.

He'd called himself the foulest of names. He'd done eight hours of work in four until his muscles cramped and his lungs all but gave out. Cursed himself all over again for a sinful lack of control.

By the time he'd stopped by Wattchel's place, he'd been spoiling for a fight and even that hadn't worked out. Stacy's whiskey-soaked landlord had been as surly as ever. What he hadn't been was stupid enough to give Boyd an excuse to use his flabby gut as a punching bag again.

"How are you feeling?" he asked when she turned to look at him again, her face flushed a delicate pink from the oven's heat.

"Amazingly strong," she murmured, lifting her chin. "And very clean. I soaked for a good hour in your tub." She gave a self-conscious laugh that seemed to run over his heated skin like a cooling breeze. "It was marvelously indulgent. I loved it."

His mind wrapped around an image of her small, fecund body immersed in bubbles, her creamy skin sheened by the rising steam and her sleek legs drawn up to give him room to slip into the bath with her.

Suddenly he didn't know what to do with his hands so he shoved them deep into his back pockets. "I...uh, stopped by your place and picked up the things Wattchel hadn't had time to sell."

Pleasure flashed in her eyes as she darted a gaze to the carton. "Oh, you brought my pictures. And the afghan!" she cried, moving past him to lift the soft woolen blanket from the box. "It's the first thing I made for the baby." She curved her lips into a smile that showed off the small dimple he'd been trying to forget. "Actually the *only* thing so far."

When she brushed her cheek against the bright wool and murmured a small sound of deep pleasure, he felt his body stir. She looked healthier than he'd ever seen her looking. The bruises were scarcely noticeable beneath her lush lower lashes, and her skin had lost the pallor of fatigue and trauma. Still slightly damp, her hair was piled in a shimmering cloud on top of her head, escaping the pins here and there to trail in wispy tendrils to her slender shoulders. His mouth went dry at the thought of tracing those sleek, dark curls with his tongue as he breathed in the exotic scent of her skin.

Suddenly starved for air, he inhaled deeply and worked at reining in his unruly urges. "Wattchel sold most everything else. Got more for it than you owed. The rest is yours. Nearly two hundred dollars. In cash."

He took ten folded twenties from the pocket of his T-shirt and held them out. "Sorry it's not more."

"It's a fortune," she said, her eyes shining beneath thick feathery lashes. "Enough for diapers and baby clothes." She was about to tuck the bills into the pocket of the slacks he'd taken from her closet only a few days ago when a look of doubt crept into her eyes. "Are you sure this is from Wattchel?"

"Scout's honor." Boyd held up three fingers, glad that he'd perfected his poker face at an early age.

She cocked her head and studied him like a militant kitten

confronted with a new challenge. "Were you really a Scout?" she demanded dubiously.

He nodded. "Until I got kicked out for fighting." Fighting, hell. He'd creamed Johnny Melrose a good one for making fun of the way he looked in the secondhand uniform that was too short and too tight.

"In that case, I accept," she said with a new lilt in her voice. "Which means I can now afford to pay you rent."

Boyd stiffened. Damn, he hadn't thought of that. "Forget it."

"Let's see, what would be fair?" She ran her tongue over her bottom lip, and he wanted to feel that clever little tongue on every inch of his naked body. Knowing that he never would put an edge on his temper.

"Stacy, I said no. I'm not going to take your money."

Stacy heard the snarl in his voice and ignored it. "How about fifty dollars a month? Plus I'll pay my share of the groceries."

Boyd felt his teeth grind. "No."

"Okay, sixty, but that's my final offer." Blithely she peeled off three twenties, folded them neatly and stuffed them back into the breast pocket of his shirt. The rest of the money she put in her own pocket.

His jaw turned hard. "This is *not* what we agreed on last night."

"Have it your way, then. I'll just go and pack up the things I unpacked." She started to turn toward the living room but found her way blocked by a solid barrier of muscle and sinew snugged suddenly against her belly. She drew back, but not before she'd felt molten heat spreading through her.

"Have you always been so set on getting your own way, or is this something you've worked up to drive me crazy?" he drawled. It was less a question than a succinct assessment, accompanied by that same lazy smile that tugged at some deep inner chord.

"Isn't that calling the kettle black?"

"I'm not—"

"Of course, you are," she said in her most soothing tone.

"Otherwise, I'd still be sitting in a perfectly charming room at the Budget Motel, watching the cockroach races."

He blinked, then glowered. "What's wrong with this place?"

"Nothing that a little healthy clutter wouldn't fix."

He shot her an insulted look before giving the gleaming kitchen a fast glance. "Looks fine to me," he declared, jutting his chin.

Stacy felt laughter bubbling, but managed to keep a straight face. "It's too...antiseptic, but then I suppose that's only normal in a doctor's house."

"Carpenter."

"Yes, of course." Stacy offered him an angelic smile before checking the clock on the stove. Seeing that the pizza was nearly ready, she opened a drawer and pointed. "See what I mean? Even your pot holders are arranged with geometric precision."

He uttered a word that had her laughing as she drew out a couple of pads. "I'll make you a deal, MacAuley. You let me mess up your cabinets and I'll let you boss me around—within reason, of course."

She heard a rumble in his chest an instant before he laughed. "I think I'm in over my head here," he muttered before plucking the hotpads from her fingers. "Go sit down. I'll serve the damn pizza."

Stacy felt like singing as she did what she'd been told. Wonder of wonders, her somber knight had actually laughed.

"Stacy, I don't expect you to pack me a lunch. Doing the books is enough for you right now."

Hearing a note of disapproval in Boyd's scratchy voice, Stacy glanced up from the jelly she was slathering over the thick layer of peanut butter already on the bread and offered him her cheeriest morning smile. Which wasn't saying much, considering she had always been—and would forever be—a night person.

So was Boyd, she'd discovered after three nights in his house. In the wee hours of the morning, while she lay in his bed reading one of his books and sipping the chamomile tea he'd taken to producing by the gallons just for her, she'd heard him prowling the other rooms.

"After spending an entire week trying to decipher your handwriting, I need a change of pace," she countered with an amused sigh.

Brow creased, he shot her a worried glance, the coffeepot he'd just lifted from the coffeemaker's hot plate poised halfway to the Thermos on the counter.

"Look, if it's too much for you, just say so. That stuff has been in that shoebox for months as it is. A couple more days or even weeks won't matter."

Stacy noticed a look of weariness around his smoky eyes and frowned. "Boyd, all I've done so far is sit at that ridiculous little desk in the living room, making piles of papers."

He poured coffee into the Thermos until it was full, then returned the nearly empty pot to the hot plate before reminding her brusquely, "Jarrod prescribed plenty of rest."

"Which I'm getting."

His frown grew even more intimidating and Stacy pictured him in the OR, glowering at the surgical techs over his mask. It hurt her to think of the skills he'd worked so hard to perfect, skills that became rustier with each day that passed.

"No stairs, no long trips, no stress."

Stacy sighed, knife poised. "Boyd, are we going to have this discussion every morning? Because if we are—"

"You're dripping."

Stacy blinked. "What?"

Boyd nodded toward the counter, one side of his mouth curling into that half grin she was beginning to love. "Jelly."

Frowning, she glanced down in time to catch a dollop of jam on her finger. Boyd reached for a towel, but before he could hand it to her, she lifted her finger to her mouth and licked it clean.

Biting off a moan, Boyd turned his back to her and busied himself replacing the lid on the Thermos. Behind the button fly of his jeans, his body was hot and hard. No matter how many ways he tried to deny it or how many names he called himself when he couldn't, he wanted her.

Even now, with the day scarcely begun and sleep still heavy in her eyes, he ached to slip his hands under the thin cotton robe draping her full breasts and ripe belly so enticingly. He wanted to touch the warm silk of her pale skin so badly his hands trembled with the effort to restrain himself. He wanted to taste her mouth and breathe in her scent, to sheathe himself in sweet heat. To drown in her.

Because he could do none of those things without destroying them both, he hadn't been able to sleep more than a few hours a night before waking in a sweat, his heart beating wildly, his hunger a fierce ache that left him raw.

"Boyd?" Stacy's voice was soft with a whisper of a tremor, reminding him that she was still fragile. Still healing.

"Yeah?" He gave the plastic lid another savage twist and stared through the window at the morning haze.

"I thought I'd work at the kitchen table today instead of the desk. If you don't mind." Stacy slipped a small bag of cookies into the sack that already contained three sandwiches and an apple before turning toward him.

"Suit yourself."

"If you leave your checkbook, I can write out the checks to the lumberyard and the electrical supply wholesaler, then you can sign them tonight."

"My company checks are in the desk, bottom left drawer."

Stacy gnawed at her lower lip as she stared at the rigid line of his sculpted shoulders and curled her hands into fists to keep from running them over the knotted muscles.

"Is there anything else that needs immediate attention?"

"No." She saw his chest lift, heard a sudden tearing sound as he drew breath. He was a man in torment, and it was her fault.

"Yes, damn it," he said, turning to face her. "We need to set some ground rules before this thing gets out of hand."

Stacy blinked. "What...*thing* do you mean, exactly?"

He glanced down at the scarred toes of his boots, ran his hands through his hair and braced his shoulders before looking at her again. "I've made some stupid mistakes in my life, but thinking I'd be able to stop with a few kisses is one of the worst."

"That bad, huh?" she murmured when his mouth drew into a firm line and his eyes narrowed.

"Try frustrating as holy hell." There was just enough wry humor in his tone to take the edge off the tension that had suddenly filled her.

"I don't recall asking you to stop kissing me." She kept her tone light. "In fact, I distinctly remember telling you how much I enjoyed being kissed by you. And I thought you enjoyed it, too."

"Too damn much."

She couldn't help laughing. "So?"

"So the last thing you need right now is sex."

"Aha. I thought that was the 'thing' you were talking about. And for the record, if Dr. Jarrod gave his okay, I wouldn't say no to you."

His mouth flattened into an intimidating line. "Why me, Stacy? Because you think you owe me?"

She tamped down an instinctive surge of indignation. "You know better than that."

"Do I? Funny, I thought we'd met only two weeks ago."

The caustic drawl in his voice was designed to hurt. And it did. "I assume, then, that you make it a practice to kiss every woman you meet."

Color rose to stain his chiseled cheekbones. "The last woman I kissed before you was my wife."

Stacy looked into his suddenly bleak gray eyes and ached with a need to comfort him. "Boyd, it's all right to be human," she said softly, closing the distance between them.

"Don't," he said, his voice strangled.

"Don't what?" She lifted both hands to frame his face. "Don't make you feel? Don't make you care?"

"I can't give you what you want."

"What I *want* is for you to forgive yourself for being alive." She stretched upward until her mouth was only inches from his. "You don't deserve this purgatory you've created for yourself."

His eyes changed, and her breath caught. "Look, if things were different…"

"Make them different."

"How? By pretending I can give you the happy ending you deserve?"

"Boyd, I know that you loved Karen. I loved Len, too. But they're gone, both of them. Terribly, tragically, yes. But also irrevocably. Cutting ourselves off from the comfort we could offer one another won't bring them back."

"Stacy—"

"Hold me, Boyd. Please." Needing his strength, she pressed closer until she was molded intimately against him, so close she felt his body trembling, so close she sensed the moment his defenses started to crumble.

"This is a mistake," he murmured an instant before he brought his arms around her, his prodigious strength gentled by the cautious slowness with which he moved. She sensed he held himself back by sheer force of will alone. On a thick moan of surrender, he brought his mouth that last inch to hers.

His lips were soft, barely skimming hers in a featherlike caress that was more a plea than a demand. Yet she felt the tension in him, tasted it on his lips, a tension she felt skittering and bunching inside her own body. Needing to be closer, she locked her hands around the thick, muscled column of his neck. The texture of his hair beneath her fingertips made her think of raw silk, warmed by the masculine heat radiating from his skin. She clung to his strength as he slowly, inexorably deepened the pressure of his mouth until she eagerly opened hers.

Boyd felt her yield, felt her tongue touch his in a shy, sweet invitation. He fought a need to crush her hard against his suddenly rigid body. It hurt to want this much and, for an instant, he couldn't breathe. It was as though he were drowning in her, her scent, her taste, the soft pressure of her breasts against his chest.

Unable to resist, he slid his tongue between her lips and

tasted. The hot welcome of her mouth sent spears of hunger gouging deep, yet he reined the worst of his need. Flattening one hand, he stroked the sensuous curve of her back, feeling the tiny shivers running over her skin beneath the nubby robe.

He slid his hands lower, cupping the intimate flare of her hips, and he heard her moan. Her tongue moved in rhythm with his, her breathing hitching, the soft sounds in her throat telling him that she was as lost as he was. When she arched harder against him, he felt an explosion of hot sensation, as much pleasure as pain as his engorged flesh responded. Try as he might, he couldn't contain the groan that slipped from his mouth to hers.

Her answering murmurs left him feeling humble and aroused at the same time. Yet he made himself ease backward until he could skim his palms over the sides of her breasts. With hands that shook he eased aside the soft rolled lapels of her robe and grazed his fingertips over her breasts, his touch as light as a whisper.

Unable to control her body's response, Stacy shivered, her nipples growing harder with every touch of his blunt fingertips. Slowly, in concert with the slow thrusts of his tongue, he stroked her breasts, then rubbed the turgid crests in a wildly erotic massage.

He freed one hand and let it slide lower, over her swollen belly, palming the contours he found wonderfully arousing. So sweet, so familiar.

Guilt hit him hard, like a hot blade to the gut. It should be Karen he was kissing, Karen who was responding with such sweet fire to each stroke of his hand, Karen whose belly was pressed so intimately against his. He pulled back, his breathing ragged.

Lost in a haze, it took Stacy a moment to realize that the callused hands that had been giving her such sweet pleasure were now wrapped around her arms, pushing her away.

"No, I won't go through that hell again," he said harshly, his face ravaged by a pain that jerked her free of her own pleasure and into a pain of her own. "Loving someone hurts too damn much.'' Without another word, he grabbed his Thermos and fled.

By midafternoon, Stacy had developed a whopper of a headache. And her eyes burned from the strain of trying to decipher Boyd's handwriting. Like many left-handed people, he wrote with a pronounced back slant, the slashing consonants and aggressive vowels all looking alike. His signature was even worse.

"If I had any sense, I'd demand a raise," she muttered, throwing down her pencil. If she had any sense, she would pack her meager belongings and walk out of his house before he took another slice from her heart.

Straightening, she let out a long sigh before pushing away from the table. It was time for her afternoon snack of fruit and yet another glass of milk. She was halfway to the refrigerator when someone knocked on the back door.

Puzzled, she eased it open to find Prudy on the doorstep, a bakery box in her hand. "Friendly Neighbors calling," she said in a singsong voice before offering Stacy a dimpled grin. "Offer me a cup of coffee and I might be persuaded to share."

Stacy leaned forward and sniffed longingly. "Please tell me I smell brownies."

"From the health food store, made with carob instead of chocolate, but still sinfully rich." Prudy cocked a coppery eyebrow. "Interested?"

"If I were Catholic, I'd badger the Pope into making you a saint," Stacy replied as she stepped back to allow the other woman to enter.

"Hmm. Saint Prudence. It does have a nice ring to it, doesn't it?" Clearly off duty, Prudy breezed past, a colorful blur in her hot pink shorts and a Hawaiian shirt garish enough to glow in the dark. Her feet were bare, and the distinct scent of suntan lotion clung to her.

"I'll make the coffee, you get the plates," Stacy ordered as she closed the door.

Ten minutes later they were sitting across from each other, blissfully munching. "When I ran into Boyd yesterday morn-

ing, he said you were putting his books in order," Prudy said
before taking a sip of coffee. In deference to Jarrod's orders
to limit her intake of caffeine, Stacy's coffee was mostly milk.

"Let's say I'm giving it the old college try."

Prudy reached for another brownie and nodded sagely.
"You have my deepest sympathy." She grinned. "I've spent
a few frustrating moments of my own trying to decipher
Boyd's scribbles."

"At the hospital?"

"Yep." Prudy bit into the brownie, then wiped crumbs
from her chin. "Unbelievable as it seems, his isn't the worst
I've seen, but close. Of course, if he'd stayed in medicine, I
have a feeling it would have gotten worse real fast."

"Does he miss it, do you think? Being a doctor."

"Only the way you and I would miss breathing."

Stacy broke off a bit of brownie and put it in her mouth.
The carob flavor suddenly tasted flat. "Do you think he'll ever
go back?"

Prudy knitted her forehead and stared down at the tabletop
for a long moment before challenging Stacy with a look. "I
think that's up to you," she said softly. "Or rather, you and
that sweet baby you're carrying."

Stacy blinked. "I'm not sure I—"

"Understand." Prudy sighed. "Yeah, I know. My ex used
to tell me I tended to make these conversational leaps. Drove
him crazy, which I suspect is one of the reasons he chose the
police force over our marriage."

Stacy heard the whisper of pain in her friend's voice and
discerned that the divorce hadn't been Prudy's idea. "Your
husband is a cop?"

"*Ex-husband*, as of five years ago this December. And yes,
last I heard, he was heading up a task force dealing with gang
warfare. Which is why I felt an instant empathy when I heard
your story."

"Yes, policemen's wives do tend to stick together." Stacy
rubbed the handle of her mug with her thumb. "Speaking of
which, I've been thinking about going back to Wenatchee
Falls when Dr. Jarrod gives me the okay to travel. I have

several friends there who would put me up until I can retrench financially.''

''Don't you dare!'' Prudy exclaimed, then grimaced. ''Sorry, that came out wrong. What I meant to say was that I would hate to see you leave, especially now, which brings us back to the subject of Boyd McAuley and the practice of medicine.''

''It does?''

Prudy nodded. ''Conversational leaps, remember?''

''Ah, I see what you mean,'' Stacy replied, laughing. ''Or rather what your ex meant.''

''You see, it's like this, Stacy. For three years, Boyd's been going to work pounding nails, coming home to work in the yard or on his truck until dark, then going to bed. Exhausted and alone.'' She exhaled heavily. ''I can't tell you how many times I've invited him to dinner or to a movie. Strictly as a buddy, you understand, which he knows as well as I do. But he always has an excuse.''

''Maybe he likes being alone.''

''Maybe. Or maybe I need to change my deodorant.'' Prudy's pixie grin came and went. ''Seriously, he's been like a zombie since...well, since the day he walked out of the OR that last time and went straight to the chief of surgery to turn in his resignation.''

Something in Prudy's tone had Stacy's stomach clenching. ''Something happened during the operation?''

Prudy pressed her finger to a crumb on her plate, then nibbled the morsel from her finger before answering. ''The patient was an accident victim, a coed from California whose car had skidded in the rain. Boyd was halfway through the operation to remove her spleen when he went dead white and just...froze. The OR tech told me she'd never seen such a look of anguish in anyone's eyes.''

Stacy sat there with a gooey lump of brownie in her mouth, suddenly unable to swallow. ''But why—''

''Apparently the patient looked a lot like Karen.'' Prudy swallowed and bit her lip. When she continued, her voice was solemn and sad. ''Everyone had been saying how brave Boyd was, returning to work only a couple of weeks after the accident. How stoic he was. And strong."

Stacy realized she had a death grip on her mug and made her fingers relax. "Instead of dealing with his emotions, he stuffed them?" she guessed softly.

"Exactly." Prudy took a sip of coffee, then made a face and got up to add hot to the cold. "Except for the rage," she said, returning to her chair. "At himself, mostly. For not saving Karen and the baby."

Stacy stared at the pattern of dappled sunlight on the gleaming surface of the oak table and fought back a sudden urge to weep. "He told me about the night of the accident."

Surprise glinted in Prudy's eyes. "I was on duty when he and Karen were brought in. I think all of us knew she wasn't going to make it."

"How terrible for you," Stacy murmured. The brownies she'd devoured with such greedy pleasure had become a lump in her stomach, and her headache had taken on jagged edges.

"Boyd never cried, you know," Prudy continued in hushed tones. "Not at the hospital, not at the funeral. Not even when he tore up the nursery." Prudy glanced inquiringly across the table, and Stacy nodded.

"I thought it was Boyd's office."

"So it's still a mess?"

Stacy shuddered at the memory. "Like a war zone."

Prudy nodded. "An appropriate term, I think, considering that Boyd nearly lost the battle for sanity in that room."

"Oh, God."

Prudy cleared her throat. "I was just coming home from work when I heard what sounded like glass shattering. I was worried, so I let myself in with the key Karen had given me ages before. I found Boyd in the baby's room." Prudy's face went waxen as she recalled the moment. "He was like a wild man. He hadn't shaved in days and he looked gaunt, as though he'd lost weight. His hands were shredded from the things he'd broken and his eyes... God, I've never seen such suffering in anyone's eyes. I tried to stop him, but he didn't hear me." Prudy drew a shaky breath before lifting her mug to her lips. "When there wasn't anything else to break, he walked past me as though I wasn't even there. He was gone for weeks. Just disappeared. When he came back, he was skinny as a rail and his eyes were old, like they are now sometimes."

"Did he say where he'd been?"

"No, and I didn't ask. I was just glad to see him." Prudy's gaze met hers, and Stacy needed her understanding.

"You care for Boyd, don't you? I mean, really care?" Prudy asked.

Does loving a man with your heart and soul count as caring? Stacy wondered. "Yes, very much."

"Then stay. Let him take care of you, fuss over you, if that's what he wants to do, see you though your delivery."

And then what? Walk away as though they'd never met, with her heart breaking more with every step? "You're thinking it would be some kind of catharsis for him?"

Prudy's face lit up. "Exactly."

Stacy bit her lip and thought about the blaze of need she'd seen in Boyd's eyes, even as he'd pushed her away.

*Love hurts too damn much.* Yet, before he'd uttered those words, she'd felt the need in him. The hunger.

Did his soul hunger with the same intensity as his body? Hunger to be whole again? To use his skills and his compassion in ways that had to have meant a great deal to him once?

"If I thought my staying would make a difference—"

"It will! Trust me, you're exactly what Boyd McAuley needs right now." Prudy gulped down the rest of her coffee before bouncing to her feet. "Now that that's settled, I have to get back to work. I'm ripping out cabinets today."

"I'd offer to exchange jobs with you, but I doubt Dr. Jarrod would approve."

"Or Boyd."

Sighing, Stacy got to her feet with her usual difficulty, bringing a sympathetic smile her way.

"How much longer do you have? Six weeks?"

"Five."

"Piece of cake with Boyd hovering over you like a mother hen."

Stacy glared at Prudy's waistline, feeling frumpy and awkward. "Uh-huh. And this from a woman who can't weigh more than a hundred pounds soaking wet."

"The product of good genes and a tendency to worry," Prudy acknowledged as Stacy opened the door to let her out.

"You're a good friend," Stacy told her as they exchanged hugs.

"So are you." Prudy turned to go, only to nearly stumble over a yellow kitten that had suddenly appeared seemingly from nowhere. "Oops, sorry, kitty."

"Well, aren't you darling?" Stacy murmured, stooping awkwardly to extend her hand to the miniature yellow tabby. The tiny creature rubbed against her fingers before curling around to lick her hand with a dainty pink tongue.

"You'll find a bag of dry cat food and a couple of bowls under the sink," Prudy said, stepping over their furry visitor.

Squinting against the sun, Stacy slanted her a look. "I didn't know Boyd had a cat."

"He doesn't. He just has this way of attracting strays. Sometimes I think there's a sign down on the highway that only felines can read. 'This way to the world's biggest softie.'"

Stacy rubbed the thick fur behind the kitten's ears and was rewarded by a sudden rumbling purr. "Are you lost, little one? Or just out for an afternoon adventure?"

"Don't get too attached to it," Prudy warned, leaning over to smooth a hand over the soft yellow pelt. "Boyd never keeps his little freeloaders for more than a few days."

Stacy felt a chill. "Please don't tell me he takes them to the pound!"

"Not a chance! He always finds them a good home." Prudy straightened, her bright hair glinting like flame in the bright sunshine. "See ya later," she said before heading toward a break in the hydrangea hedge.

Smiling, Stacy lifted the kitten and rubbed her face in the soft fur. The kitty batted at her cheek with a paw before letting out a contented meow.

"Let's see, what should we call you?"

"Stacy?" Prudy called from next door. "Don't name the cat!"

"It's too late," Stacy called back. "She already told me her name. It's Sunshine."

# Eleven

Stacy was stretched out in a sun lounger she'd borrowed from Prudy, enjoying the shade provided by a gnarled oak in the backyard, when she heard Boyd's truck pull into the carport.

"It's okay, Sunny," she murmured to the kitten snuggled down for a nap on her bare thighs. "He frowns a lot, but he really has an incredibly soft heart in that big chest."

Sunshine twitched her furry ears and opened one eye, as though registering her doubts. Stacy laughed softly as she smoothed her hand over the kitten's dainty little back.

"We're over here," she called as Boyd headed up the walk toward the back door, looking preoccupied and tired. The man could make a fortune modeling jeans, she thought. Or anything else, she amended, eyeing the impressive girth of his tanned biceps beneath the rolled sleeves of his plain cotton shirt. Her unpredictable libido started revving at high speed, making her suddenly short of breath.

"We?" he asked, veering off the walk onto the grass toward the shadowed spot. His hair was nicely mussed, hinting at the towheaded rascal he must have been once, but she suspected it had been a long time since those topaz dark eyes had been lit with mischief. Too long.

"Boyd, meet Sunshine," she said, lifting one of the kitty's tiny paws when Boyd stopped a few feet away. "Sunny for short."

"Oh Lord, not another one," he muttered, shaking his head. The dark mood of this morning seemed to have passed, and she let out a relieved breath.

"Prudy said you have a knack of attracting strays."

Boyd hesitated, then crouched down next to the chair and extended a finger toward the cat. "Cute little beggar," he muttered, trying not to smile at the sudden glint of curiosity in the kitten's bright eyes.

"I fed her some of the cat food you keep under the sink," Stacy told him with a smile he'd give a small fortune to taste.

She was wearing drawstring shorts patterned with wild geometric shapes that he was pretty sure he'd seen Prudy wearing a time or two, and one of the shirts he'd packed for her. Both were anything but provocative, but he felt his blood pressure spiking nevertheless. He withdrew his hand, conscious that the kitten was stretched across perfect thighs that looked touchably silky.

"How are you feeling?" He figured he'd be safe concentrating his attention on her face. He was wrong. Try as he might, he couldn't help noticing the ripe curve of the lips he'd tasted only a few hours ago. Couldn't keep from remembering the satiny feel of those lips against his. Couldn't help remembering his own clumsy rejection of all that she'd been offering.

"Actually, I'm feeling as pampered and lazy as Sunny here," she murmured with a blissful sigh. "Prudy brought brownies and Linda next door dropped off a casserole that smells like heaven itself. Apparently she and Prudy have formed a conspiracy of kindness."

Boyd glanced toward the Ladds' bungalow. A tidy row of diapers hung from the clothesline Marshall had put up at Linda's insistence when the twins were born the day after Christmas. A militant environmentalist, Linda recycled everything.

"I like your friends," Stacy said softly, claiming his attention again. "And they're very protective of you. Prudy's already warned me not to fall in love with you, and Linda pretty much said the same thing, only in different words."

She saw the frown start in his eyes a split second before he drew his bold brows together. "Seems to me they're being more protective of you than me."

"But there's no need of that, is there?" she said with a comfortable smile. "You're not interested in a relationship with me, and I was certainly too well brought up to push myself on a man who doesn't want me."

"Damn it, Stacy, it's not—"

"Boyd, it's okay." She laid a hand on his arm where it rested on one knee. Beneath her touch, his muscles turned to cabled steel. "I understand how you feel and why. You don't want to fall in love with me, and you don't want me to fall in love with you. Fair enough. I'll do my best not to, although I warn you it's going to be difficult, given the fact that I already like you a lot, not to mention being wildly attracted to your gorgeous body." She sighed and rolled her eyes before assuming a prim tone. "Be that as it may, however, since you insist on my staying in your house, I suggest we keep our interactions strictly platonic."

Boyd felt an odd emotion take hold of him. He told himself it was relief. "Works for me," he said, getting to his feet. He was about to offer to bring her a cold drink when she held out a small hand.

"Then it's a deal," she declared with a smile full of whimsy and spunk—and pride.

"Yeah, sure." He took her hand in his and felt her fingers mold around his for an instant before they stiffened into a businesslike shake.

"Now if you'll kindly give a little tug to help me up," she said with perfect composure, "I'll go put that marvelous crab dish of Linda's into the oven."

Well, hell! Boyd thought as he ducked his head under the shower spray and let the water pound on the knotted muscles at the back of his neck. So much for the diplomatic speech he'd been rehearsing damn near all afternoon. About how he didn't want to hurt her any more than she'd been hurt. And how they should keep things on a strictly friendship basis. Platonic. Just like the lady said, an inner voice taunted. Cut his good intentions right off at the knees.

So how come he was feeling like he'd just taken a right cross to the jaw?

Because he was an idiot, he thought as he lifted his face to the needle-sharp spray. An idiot who'd just condemned himself to five weeks of the fires of hell.

Over the next few weeks, they learned to live with each other.

Stacy learned never to feed him liver or talk about his years in medicine. Boyd learned to keep his distance in the morning until she'd downed the one cup of black coffee Luke Jarrod allowed her.

Boyd bought a cellular phone and pinned the number next to each phone, along with Jarrod's at home and work. A few days later he started wearing a beeper again and that number, too, he added to the list.

Whenever they were discussing current events or business matters, they were perfectly comfortable with each other. But whenever one of them trespassed on the rules they'd tacitly set up, the attraction between them seethed and bubbled like simmering water about to boil.

By unspoken agreement she waited until he'd left for the day before showering. He showered at night, while she was watching television or visiting with Prudy next door.

Stacy cooked and he cleaned up. No matter how careful she might be, or how cautious he was about his movements, they couldn't help bumping into each other in the tiny kitchen. Or brushing hands when she passed him a plate to wash.

After a week of stiff tension and even stiffer apologies from one or the other, Boyd had tersely suggested she relax in the living room while he finished up. One look at the hot hunger in his eyes had sent her scooting for the sofa as soon as the meal was ended.

Things were better then. To Stacy's delight she discovered that Boyd shared her passion for baseball, and they spent hours debating the finer points. As a kid Boyd had followed the San Francisco Giants and had played center field like his idol, Willie Mays.

Stacy herself had been partial to Johnny Bench of the Cincinnati Reds, a bush leaguer compared to Willie, Boyd had scoffed one night while they'd shared a bowl of popcorn and watched a Mariners game on the tube. If Mays hadn't played in a ballpark perched practically in the middle of San Francisco Bay where the wind blew in from center field, he damn well would have hit as many homers as Aaron.

Stacy had disagreed vehemently, more to watch Boyd's usually wary eyes take on a passionate glow as he waxed almost poetic over the sweetness of Willie's swing and his grace in the field.

He seemed to like talking to her about baseball and other things, too—like the trouble he'd been having replicating a piece of gingerbread trim he'd recommended to the Gilmartins and the satisfaction he'd felt when he'd finally mastered the intricate pattern. Or the problem getting the house's cranky old dumbwaiter to work again.

It didn't take her long to realize that Boyd demanded a standard very close to perfection in the work he did—and in himself. When he fell short, his frustration and self-contempt were painful to see. Whenever possible, she made suggestions for some minor improvement or other and was ridiculously pleased when he praised her ingenuity.

Twice since she'd settled into his house almost a month ago, he'd taken her to dinner at D'Agostino's Old World Ristorante where the checkered tablecloths were always clean and the atmosphere soothingly casual. To thank her for solving a nagging problem, he'd told her with an offhand shrug that she suspected masked a concern that she was working too hard to untangle his convoluted bookkeeping system.

The third time they'd shown up, owner Mario D'Agostino had greeted them with a satisfied wink, as well as his usual grin. The stocky transplanted Italian and his tall, slender wife,

Sofia, lived above the restaurant with their four little ones. According to Boyd, Sofia too was one of Luke Jarrod's patients. Their last baby, an adorable little bambino with his father's soulful brown eyes, had just turned eight months old.

"I have just said to Sofia that it is again Wednesday evening and so I expect to see my friend Boyd and his lovely lady," Mario said when he had seated them at the table by the window. The best in the house, he'd told them the first time he'd smiled Stacy to her seat at the padded banquette.

Even though Boyd had taken great pains to introduce her as a friend who was helping out with his bookkeeping, it was clear to Stacy that Mario wanted to believe his friend Boyd was head over heels in love. Stacy knew better. In his mind she was simply another stray kitten to be looked after until it was safe for her to be on her own again.

"Is Mario Junior still teething?" Stacy asked as she scooted backward as far as she could in order to make more room for her swollen belly.

"And how!" Mario rolled his eyes. "All night he cries, that one. First I walk with him and then Sofia."

"Did you try whiskey on his gums?"

Mario nodded, sighed. "First whiskey, then Chianti. The poor little one, he only cried louder. So I finished the wine myself, and the baby's crying didn't seem so loud." His grin flashed white against his olive skin as he opened a menu with a Latin flourish and set it before her. "The linguine with clam sauce has been blessed by the angels."

"That's a good enough recommendation for me," Stacy declared without even sparing a glance at the menu. "And a double order of antipasto with—"

"Extra peppers," Mario finished for her, his eyes sparkling as they met hers for an instant before shifting across the table. "I'll fix up a carton to go for you so you won't have to come knocking on my door at midnight," he told Boyd with a grin.

Stacy saw the color rising in Boyd's neck and felt her jaw drop. "You didn't?" she questioned, her gaze seeking Boyd's across the gleaming white tablecloth.

"First line of self-defense," he muttered, lifting his water glass to his mouth and taking a long swallow. "So you wouldn't be opening and closing cupboards in the middle of the night."

Stacy took in air, half annoyed, half beguiled at the thought of Boyd running out at night to replenish the jar of peppers she kept next to his collection of coffee mugs. "I offered to sleep on the couch," she reminded him a bit astringently.

"Don't start that again," he muttered, closing the menu with a snap that reminded her Mario was still hovering. "I'll have the special."

"Good choice, my old friend." Mario beamed. "And the usual glass of Chianti?"

Boyd nodded. Scowled. Shifted position. He was wearing a shirt she'd ironed for him over his strenuous objections, and slacks for once, instead of jeans. As usual, he'd brushed his hair with his fingers, and though it was shiny and clean, any real styling had been left to chance. It gave him a windblown look she found utterly irresistible.

"And for my lovely new friend, milk, as always?" Mario turned to Stacy and his smile seemed fashioned to reassure and approve. Nodding, Stacy returned his smile with an inner sadness. Once Tory was born, and she herself was fully recovered, she had made up her mind to return to Wenatchee Falls.

After chatting for another moment or two, Mario picked up the menus neither had read and hurried off toward the kitchen. Stacy slipped the silverware from her napkin, then grimaced as she had trouble squeezing it between the table and her belly.

"Looks like we'll have to sit at a table next time," Boyd said, snapping open his own napkin.

"Only if the chair doesn't have arms," she said, laughing ruefully.

Their drinks and salads arrived, brought by a matronly waitress Stacy hadn't seen before. "Extra peppers?" she asked in an accent that mirrored Mario's.

"Mine," Stacy told her with a greedy smile.

While Boyd sipped his wine, she dug in, all but purring as

she bit into a hot pepper. "Your stomach is moving," he said after a moment or two. "Tory must like peppers."

Stacy glanced down. Sure enough, the kicks and punches she was feeling under her heart were clearly visible under her floppy shirt. "Dr. Jarrod says an active baby means an easy delivery. I told him I wanted that in writing."

Boyd glanced toward the next table where Mario was seating a young couple. "Other than being active...the baby's okay?"

Stacy was touched by the faint raspiness in his tone. And by the anxious look in his eyes. Every Wednesday morning she saw the doctor. Every Wednesday morning Boyd drove her to Jarrod's office. Instead of coming in with her, he waited in the truck. On the way home he asked detailed questions about her condition. This was the first time he'd asked about the baby.

"The baby's fine," she assured him, drawing his gaze to her face. "The heartbeat of a stevedore." And she, herself, was blooming. Jarrod had given her the okay to resume normal activities, with the usual caveats of what had been a routine pregnancy before her accident.

Boyd returned her smile, briefly. But the strain in his face didn't ease. It hurt to see the ambivalence in his eyes. There was too much concern there. Too much pain, too many memories.

She ached for him in ways he could never tolerate. The books she'd read about the process of grieving had all stressed the need to express, to vent. To scream and rage, if that's what was needed. To batter a pillow or a punching bag, perhaps. Or to cry until there were no more tears. According to Prudy, Boyd hadn't cried. But he had all but destroyed the room meant for his child. So perhaps he'd taken one tiny step.

The trouble was she didn't know how to help him take the next. Or in what direction he needed to go. And so she tried to make him loosen his death grip on his emotions enough to laugh. She'd even succeeded a time or two. But just when she thought he might be learning to accept a past he couldn't change, he withdrew from her as completely as though he'd stepped through a door and slammed it behind her. It hurt when he shut her out.

Worse by far, however, were those fleeting moments when he looked at her with an unguarded hunger in his eyes that stole her breath and heated her blood. Her own hunger to be in his arms again was never far from the surface of her daily routine. Even now, as she watched him lift his glass to his mouth and drink, she longed to feel that hard mouth softening over hers.

The impulse to lean forward and taste the wine lingering on his lips was nearly irresistible. Instead, she lifted her own glass. "Here's to the successful completion of the Gilmartins' remodel," she said with a smile. "I sent them the final bill this morning."

"Good thing I collected my tools yesterday," he said, touching his wineglass to her milk tumbler. "And here's to my bookkeeper, who keeps me on track." As they drank the toast, their gazes met and locked. In the restaurant's deliberately dim lighting, his eyes were as smoky as Mexican topaz. For an instant she was sure she saw more than the appreciation of an employer for a competent employee in the depths. Much more. She felt a tightness in her chest and a stirring around her heart that had nothing to do with the baby.

"What job have you decided to accept next?" she asked over the muted notes of a Puccini aria playing in the background.

His gaze flickered, then shifted to follow the waitress as she approached. "I've been giving some thought to taking a few weeks off," he said when their entrées were in front of them.

"A vacation?" she asked, picking up her fork.

He shrugged one shoulder. "Why not? June's already half over. I figured it's time."

She tasted the linguine and felt her taste buds sigh with pleasure. "Any idea where you want to go?" she asked, forking up another bite.

"Nowhere special." His tone was offhand, deliberately so, she suspected.

"Boyd, it's sweet of you to worry, but I have another two

and a half weeks before I'm due. Maybe longer, according to Dr. Jarrod."

"Yeah, so you said." He concentrated on his pasta, working his way halfway through the more-than-generous portion before glancing up again. "Guess I'm about as subtle as a Mack truck, huh."

"Just about. But I appreciate the thought." She was about to tell him she didn't need a baby-sitter when she remembered what Prudy had told her. *Let him take care of you, fuss over you, if that's what he wants to do, see you through your delivery.*

She took a sip of milk to steady herself, then glanced around until she caught Mario's eye and waved him over. "More peppers?" he asked, nodding toward the few bits of lettuce on the salad plate, all that remained of her double order of antipasto.

"Well, maybe just a few more," she said, distracted for a moment by the anticipation of the spicy, stinging taste on her tongue. Mario and Boyd exchanged identical looks, two superior males indulging the little woman's whim. She told herself she should be indignant. Instead she was touched.

Directing a smile Mario's way, she added brightly, "Also, I was wondering if I could talk you into preparing a picnic lunch for me tomorrow. My boss is taking some time off and I thought I'd treat him to a day in the woods."

# Twelve

---

**B**oyd couldn't remember the last time he'd gone on a picnic in the middle of a work week. Hell, he couldn't remember the last time he'd been on a picnic, period. But as he shoveled his hands under his head and idly watched the leaves overhead dancing in the breeze, he had to admit he was having a damned good time.

As a kid he'd never had the time to idle away an afternoon. There'd always been chores to do, siblings to watch over, schoolwork to wedge into odd moments. In college and med school, he'd been even busier. After he'd married, he'd done the things Karen liked. Symphony openings and black-tie dinners. Charity dances and opera parties. As far as he'd been concerned, they'd been little more than trumped-up excuses for the Waverlys and their crowd to dress to the nines and play grown-up.

He could still see Karen frowning in front of the bathroom mirror, trying to decide which earrings to wear. Diamond studs or pearl drops, she'd asked him once, driven almost to tears by her struggle to decide.

He remembered being half-dead from a double shift and two trauma cases, remembered the urge to grab the damn earrings and toss them down the toilet if that meant the two of them could stay home for a change. Instead, he'd mumbled something that seemed to please her.

Closing his eyes, he inhaled the air that smelled of summer heat and river water and tried to picture Karen perched on a spread ragged blanket with her shoes off and her hair flying every which way. Tried and failed.

A hothouse orchid by birth and inclination, she'd hated bugs and dirt and sweat almost as much as she'd hated the stretch marks pregnancy had gouged into her smooth, salon-pampered skin. Sometimes he thought she'd hated him for giving her a baby in the first place. Sometimes he hated himself. No, not sometimes. Most of the time. Or he had, until a pixie with smiling amber eyes and the moxie of a nineteenth-century buccaneer settled into his house.

Smiling to himself, he turned his head and tried to picture Stacy with a bandanna restraining her thick hair and a gleaming cutlass clamped in those small white teeth. Instead, he saw a woman so lovely it took his breath. A wild rose like the kind that had set down roots in this rich soil a century ago. A woman with the kind of class money couldn't buy. A survivor who could laugh through her tears and fight an army of troubles to protect her babies.

He'd never been much for sentiment. Or saying the romantic words women liked to hear. Words he suddenly wished came more easily. And yet, in a dozen lifetimes he would never be able to describe the things he felt when he looked at her. About how pretty she was, how he'd never seen a woman with a smile as appealing or hair the color of hers.

Dark brown wasn't adequate. Not with so many shades of brown and gold intermingling. Since they'd met her hair had grown longer and, when she wore it down, reached beyond her shoulders in a soft, lustrous fan that begged for a man's touch.

Because of the day's heat, she'd pulled it into a kind of ponytail that bounced playfully every time she moved her head, which she did often as she talked, and the strands that had escaped framed her face like wispy quotation marks. A face that needed not a lick of makeup to make it beautiful, he decided, his gaze lingering on a profile as fine as any museum miniature. Not even the slanting pink scar left by the accident over her dark, expressive eyebrows could mar the perfection of its oval shape.

These past weeks the time spent in the sun had erased the hospital pallor of her skin and added luster to an already perfect complexion. But it was her smile that stopped his heart and spiced his blood. Sweet or saucy by turns, it lifted his spirits and made his mouth water for a taste of those soft lips.

She was wearing Prudy's shorts again and a thin cotton shirt the color of watermelon. Her legs were bare and lightly tanned, and in spite of the ripening of her body, deliciously slender and sleek.

Lord help him, he wanted her. More and more every day. It was getting so bad he had trouble concentrating on anything more than the simplest of tasks. Like breathing.

He'd even thought about taking Marion Gilmartin's newly divorced sister up on the offer she'd made him one day last week. For dinner and "whatever" she'd said. But the thought of coming home to Stacy with another woman's perfume on his skin had stopped him cold.

"I can see why this is one of Prudy's favorite places in the whole wide world," Stacy murmured when she caught his gaze lingering too long on her face. "It's hard to believe millions of people are living just a few miles away from this spot."

Sighing happily, she turned her face up toward a thick canopy of sycamore leaves. To the west in a triangular patch of azure sky an eagle soared in solitary majesty above the meandering creek that bore his name. Hidden in a nearby thicket a sparrow celebrated her joy at the perfect day in song.

Next to her, Boyd selected another flat skipping stone from the cache she'd collected earlier. "Millions of people hard at work," he said with a brief grin before sending the stone skimming across the surface of the fast-running stream.

Stacy watched the stone hit the bank on the other side and sink from sight. In this part of Eagle Creek, the water was a clear bottle green, the result of the snow melting at the highest elevations. Close in to the grassy bank where they'd spread their blanket, the recent spring floods had gouged a deep pool where eddies swished and swirled in hypnotic fury, turning the water's surface foamy white. Behind them, thickets of willows nestled between two giant boulders provided a lacy emerald screen, hiding them from the rest of the civilized world.

Since they'd driven off the main road and onto the gravel lane Prudy had described in her meticulous directions, they'd seen a small herd of fat, smug-looking cows huddling in the shade of a huge grandfather oak, several gigantic crows lined up like disapproving sentries on a fence rail and acres of ripening blackberries—but no other living souls.

The lunch Mario had provided turned out to be enough for an entire Roman legion on a forced march, but by midafternoon they'd managed to devour all but a few pitiful remains. "Sure you don't want the last tart?" she offered over the creek's rippling music.

"Positive." Boyd shifted and sat up. "I'm fixing to bust as it is."

Stacy smoothed her shirt over her protruding belly and eyed him curiously. "Why I declare, Mr. Boyd, do I hear an echo of Southern roots in your speech?"

His laugh was wonderfully infectious—and all too rare. "My mother was from South Carolina. Her father was a logger chasing the good life and figured the Northwest would never run out of trees."

"He wasn't the only one," Stacy said with a sigh for the thousands of timber workers who'd been displaced over the past ten years by the growing lack of harvestable trees.

He acknowledged that with a grim nod. "Grandpop had enough sense to see what was happening before most of his buddies on the crew. Started to perfect his woodworking skills when I was still a kid."

He leaned forward to snag a marinated olive from the remnants of their lunch. Sunshine caught in his hair, turning it to gold. In her more idle moments she'd imagined running her fingers through that rough-and-tumble thatch.

In deference to the heat he'd worn shorts and a polo shirt, which he'd shucked as soon as they'd settled. His sneakers had been the next to go. Stacy, too, was barefoot and reveled in the feel of the cool grass against the soles of her feet.

"Is that where you learned carpentry?" she asked when his gaze flickered her way again. "From your grandfather?"

He nodded, and his mouth relaxed, stirring longings she forced herself to ignore. "He could barely write his own name, but he could find the soul in a rough piece of wood like no one I've ever known."

Stacy heard the gruff affection in his voice and smiled. "Was your father a carpenter, too?"

Boyd shook his head, and the half smile softening his mouth faded. "He didn't have the patience. Worked for a mill outside of Roseburg for thirty years before his liver turned to dog meat."

"He was an alcoholic?"

"In the end, yes. After my mother died, his one goal in life was to join her. He was bigger than most men, so it took longer than it should. But he finally managed. Bled to death internally one night, sitting next to my mother's grave." One side of his mouth moved. "My grandmother claimed it was the Irish in him that drove him to grieve himself to death."

Stacy felt a chill and hugged herself. "How old were you when your mother died?" she asked softly.

"Twelve." He picked up another stone and, with a snap of his powerful wrist, sent it screaming across the water toward a river birch on the opposite bank.

"Was it unexpected?" she asked when the loud thwack of solid granite against solid wood had faded.

"Yes, but it shouldn't have been." His jaw turned hard, and Stacy cursed herself for bringing up painful memories. "She'd just given birth prematurely to twin sons," he said in the same toneless voice he'd used when recounting his nightmare plunge into that dark ravine and its aftermath. "She and one of the babies died within hours of one another. It was touch and go with Cullen for weeks, but he hung on. And now he's taller than I am.''

Stacy pictured a younger, bigger version of Boyd, with those same wide shoulders and rock-hard torso. And a longer stretch to his muscular legs. Taller his brother might be, she decided after a moment's absorbed reflection, but she doubted very much if Cullen were stronger. Or even tougher.

"And your sisters?''

"Happily married, or so they claim.'' Suddenly restless, he stood and held out a hand. "C'mon, let's work out some kinks.''

Stacy slipped her hand into his, enjoying the hard strength of his grip and the warmth of his touch. As he pulled her effortlessly to her feet, she found herself feeling graceful instead of cumbersome for the first time in weeks.

"Thanks,'' she said, careful not to brush against him. "Position changes are a challenge these days. I tend to overbalance if I'm not careful.''

His gaze swept over her belly, warming her. "Your center of gravity has shifted.''

Stacy laughed. "I'll say. I sit on it these days.''

His laugh echoed hers as they began to wade through the sun-warmed ripples at the edge of the bank. Instead of letting go of her hand, he surprised her by interlacing their fingers until their palms met, sending a sweet shivering awareness all the way through her.

"Cold?'' he asked, watching her intently.

Amazed that he'd attuned himself to her so intimately, she shook her head and smiled. "The water feels good.'' As good as his hand felt holding hers so snugly.

"Mind the rocks,'' he cautioned when they'd gone a few more feet along the meandering watercourse. "They're slippery.''

"I like the way they feel. Like smooth, wet satin.''

His mouth slanted. "I used to fish in a creek like this one.''

"Catch anything?''

He looked so offended she laughed. "Sorry.''

He accepted her apology with a boyish grin. "Steelhead, mostly. Cooked 'em and ate 'em right by the creek."

"Because they taste better that way or because you were too hungry to wait?"

"Both." His look turned sheepish. "And because the game warden couldn't count our catch."

Laughing softly, she watched a dragonfly skimming the water's surface before veering toward a patch of clover growing almost to the creek bed itself. "Isn't that called poaching?"

"We preferred to think of it as ingenuous free enterprise."

"I'll grant you the free part," she teased, and was about to ask him who was the other half of the "we" was when her foot slipped on a mossy rock and she lurched sideways, ending up all but smashed against him. She would have fallen but for the arm he clamped around her waist.

"Oops," she murmured, glancing up at him. "Guess I wasn't watching where I was going."

"Okay now?"

"I think so." But her voice was suddenly strained and thin, bringing a frown to his mouth.

Feet braced wide, he shifted until she was snuggled against him, then brought the other arm around her. "You're driving me crazy." The rough scratch of frustration in Boyd's voice had Stacy's heart racing.

"I don't mean to," she murmured.

His mouth quirked an instant before he bent to feather a kiss beneath her ear. "Then stop wearing such a sexy perfume," he whispered against her skin. She felt a shiver starting inside and closed her eyes.

"It's just soap. The same soap you use."

"Can't be," he said, biting her ear gently while his hand shaped the curve of her spine. Stacy shivered and let the pleasure flow over her, just as the water rippled over the rocks a few feet away.

"And another thing, get rid of that slinky nightgown you've taken to wearing." His tongue made a slow, sensuous exploration of her ear before withdrawing, and she drew in breath.

"It's one of your old T-shirts," she managed to say as she

arched her neck backward. "Remember I asked if you had one I could borrow?"

He pressed his face to the hollow of her shoulder and kissed the exposed skin he found there. "Must have slipped my mind while I was trying not to think about you sitting in all those bubbles in my bathtub."

"No...bubbles," she confided before he shifted his attention to her mouth. But instead of kissing her, he touched his tongue to her lower lip, then drew back.

"You taste sweet, in spite of the peppers you eat like candy."

She felt her lips curving even as his came closer.

"Kiss me, Stacy."

"What about our deal?" she said a little breathlessly.

"Forget our deal! Put the poor, suffering fool out of his misery." His voice was laced with humor, but the look in his eyes was hot and needy.

"Only if you do the same for me," she whispered on a rush of air. Her heart was slamming against her ribs, making it difficult to breathe. He smelled like sunshine and looked like a dream come true.

His mouth aligned with hers, came down softly. Her lips were ready, aching. His kiss was gentle yet edged with fire ready to kindle. Stacy felt the world tilt as she threaded her arms around his waist and held on.

"Definitely sweet." He nibbled at her lips. pushing the tip of his tongue into the corner of her mouth, then withdrawing it, teasing her, tantalizing her, giving her time to resist.

But she couldn't pull away. Not while it felt so good to be held like this. Not while he was stroking her with such absorbing care, letting his fingers trail along her jawline.

She liked the feel of his big, hard body rubbing slowly against hers, caressing her, provoking her, and she loved the feel of his hands on her bare arms, gentling her, petting her, inviting her to put those arms around his neck.

He groaned as her hands slid over his shoulders and linked behind his head. He nuzzled her neck with his face, then kissed the tender area below her earlobe before again tracing the delicate whorls of her ear with the tip of his tongue.

Heat rocketed through her, and she rubbed against him, letting the friction of his hard chest abrade her nipples until the tiny peaks pushed hard against her shirt.

She let out a gasp of pleasure, delighting in the shower of sensations. Heat and chill, throbbing pulse and bone-melting sighs. And love, so much love she thought she would burst with it.

Her body began to hum, and then to vibrate with a primitive force, and she ran her hands over his shoulders and down his arms, pulling him closer, closer.

He took her lips, plunging his tongue between them until she was sucking on him, loving the taste and feel and wetness of him inside her mouth. She moaned helplessly.

Boyd stiffened, then broke off the kiss. "We...I swore I wouldn't do this," he whispered in a husky, choked voice. His heart was pounding in his ears and his breathing was ragged. It hurt to think. To feel. "You're almost nine months pregnant...the baby..."

"Is fine," she murmured in a low, throbbing voice that seemed to fill him with emotion.

"I could hurt you."

Stacy felt the conflict in the strong arms holding her so gently, saw the tension in the taut lines of his face. "You won't."

He groaned hoarsely and buried his face in the curve of her neck. A ragged breath shuddered through him, and his arms tightened convulsively. "I need you, Stacy. So much. Too much." The words seemed torn from him.

"I need you, too. And it hurts." At this moment she belonged to him, no matter what happened in the future.

Silently Boyd took her hand and led her to the carpet of clover. Sunlight filtered from the canopy overhead to form lacy patterns of gold against the lush green thatch.

"We'll go slowly," he promised, slipping his fingers under the long tail of her shirt. Her skin was warm and smooth, sending tendrils of need spiraling inside him.

Suddenly shy, she pressed her hands over his. "Don't expect centerfold material," she warned on a little laugh.

His eyes clouded. "Stacy, you are a beautiful woman," he said in a low throbbing tone that sent shivers running through her. "Breathtakingly, stupendously, wonderfully beautiful. And I want you so much I'm shaking with it."

"I thought you were just cold," she teased, winning a slow, sensuous smile that broke her heart.

"Anything but," he murmured.

Slowly Boyd unbuttoned her shirt and opened her bra, letting her breasts spill into his palms. The air was cool on her skin, but his lips were warm as he kissed first one hard nipple, then the other.

She gasped as his fingers slid along her sides, warm and intimate. She loved the rough feel of his skin and the careful stroking of his hands as he eased her out of her shirt and bra.

For his own pleasure, Boyd stepped back and let his gaze trail over the ripe swell of breasts and belly, his throat clogged with a need to tell her how truly lovely she was at that moment.

Instead, he flattened his hand against her belly and leaned forward to kiss the creamy flesh. He felt her shiver and glanced up to see tears in her eyes. "Oh Boyd," she whispered, her voice breaking.

Keeping his gaze on hers, he slipped out of his shorts and briefs, then eased her free of her shorts and plain cotton panties. When they were both naked, he took her into his arms again. With a blissful sigh, she settled against him, feeling as though she'd come home.

"Are you sure?" he whispered against her temple.

"Make me feel whole again," she replied, her voice trembling.

He groaned softly, and then he kissed her again. Her lips, her eyelids, her earlobe. And she kissed him, loving the taste of him.

They were both breathing hard by the time he lifted his head. Her eyes were clouded and dreamy, her lips full and rosy.

"My legs feel rubbery," she murmured, laughing.

"I think we can take care of that." Keeping his own need under tight control, he gently lowered her to the thick green blanket, then lay beside her. He dipped his head to savor the taste of her nipples on his tongue, then lapped at the darker skin surrounding them until she moaned softly. A quick look at her passion-drowsy face assured him she wasn't in pain, and he allowed himself the exquisite pleasure of caressing her belly.

Stacy felt her baby shift, then settle under the slow, loving touch of Boyd's hand, and a pleasure she had never known flooded through her. Beneath her, the grass was thick and cool, and the air was filled with the sensuous scents of summer.

"Okay?" he murmured, his gaze bathing her in his concern.

"Wonderful," she murmured, wringing a chuckle from him. Oh how she loved him, she thought, letting her eyes drift closed. His hands smoothed over her, finding every curve, every pulse point, every singing nerve ending until she was nearly crazed with wanting him. She moved restlessly, her hands reaching for him, urging him to fill her.

"Easy, honey," Boyd whispered, his own needs tearing at him like a wild thing. Gently, tenderly, he cupped his hand over the mound between her legs, kneading and stroking until she arched upward, crying out, her eyes flying open, then glazing over with a stunned pleasure.

Even as she shuddered, he braced his weight on his hands and eased into her slowly, carefully, watching her face, her eyes, the trembling of her soft lips as she murmured his name. Slowly he began to move, fighting a clawing need to take his own pleasure in one hard pounding thrust. Instead, he rocked back and forth against the velvet walls sheathing him, feeling the pleasure bunch and rush inside him, until finally he could no longer hold back.

He watched her face, murmured her name, heard her sigh his own. His release, when it came, brought tears to his eyes.

# Thirteen

----

**A** cramp in her left leg woke Stacy with a jerk, and she reached down to rub the knotted muscle, only to feel Boyd sit bolt upright next to her, his tanned body dark against the moonlit window. "What's wrong?" he demanded, his voice rust deep.

"Charley horse in my calf," she muttered, struggling to reach past her belly.

"Here, let me," he said, throwing off the sheet and reaching for her leg with one swift, determined motion. His hands were warm against her flesh, kneading gently yet with a skill born of experience and caring. She felt the painful knot relaxing and let out a relieved sigh.

"Better?"

"Mmm," she murmured, closing her eyes. In fact, it felt wonderful to have his hands on her, no matter the reason. Hands that were now stroking her leg instead of kneading tight muscles.

"Your skin looks milky in the moonlight." His voice was hushed, oddly reverent, and she felt her heart soaring.

"Yours is dark," she murmured, reaching out a hand to touch his shoulder. She felt him start, and his hand stilled. "Like rare soft leather over steel," she added, sliding her palm over the heavily padded shoulder.

His breath hissed out in a low rush as he bent forward to brush his lips over her thigh. The muscles there quivered, not from pain but from pleasure, and her heart took off on a steady gallop. His fingers followed where his mouth had been, trailing liquid fire.

"You smell like ripe peaches," he murmured, warming her skin with his breath. "Ready for eating." He nipped at her flesh, then swirled over the tiny imprint of his teeth with his tongue.

Stacy felt her breath shudder out of her in a long drawn-out moan that had him glancing up at her. "Easy, honey. This is just the beginning."

His fingers trailed higher, to the lace of the gown he'd packed for her all those weeks ago.

"Beginning?" she asked before another wave of pleasure ran over her.

"Since we're both so wide-awake, I figure we should put the time to good use." Slowly his palm moved over the full curve of her hip. "Unless you'd rather go back to sleep."

Stacy drew a breath and pretended to consider, but when his fingers tightened against her softly yielding flesh, her answer came out in a ragged moan.

Boyd shifted until he was lying next to her. He kissed her shoulder before easing her to her side. His chest was warm against her back.

"I love touching you. Your skin is as smooth as this pretty little scrap of satin." His voice was a whisper in the silvery moonlight, mingling with the rush of her breathing while he trailed his fingertips over the thin material of her gown where it draped her belly, then moved lower to her thighs and back once more. The slow, lingering caresses were punctuated by the gentle nipping of his teeth at her nape, her shoulder, the soft flesh of her arm.

Each time his hand traveled back up her body, he brushed

the throbbing mound between her thighs, each stroke moving higher, until finally he trailed his fingers in a slow, sensuous figure eight around her full breasts. Her nipples tingled, distended, already aching for the hot, moist possession of his mouth, and she moaned. Gently, slowly, he eased closer until she was cradled against him, his hard thighs nuzzling hers. His arousal was hot and thick against her buttocks, so close to the moist sheath throbbing to welcome him.

Stacy's breath unraveled into broken sighs as Boyd's hand moved slowly from one breast to the other, caressing her, cherishing her. When his finger slid beneath the lacy hem of her gown and moved upward, she held her breath.

"More?" he whispered hoarsely.

She managed a keening sound of assent that had him groaning.

He skimmed a hand over the tops of her thighs before touching the tight coils of silky hair between her legs. No longer able to lie still, she moved restlessly, and the motion rubbed soft flesh against hard, wringing a groan from him that sent shafts of pleasure slicing through her. Without stopping to think, she undulated against him, feeling the demanding heat of his arousal burning her skin.

The instant, fierce slam of need that went through Boyd took his breath and dammed the sudden groan in his throat. She was so soft, so womanly, so utterly giving. He felt humbled and fiercely protective at the same time.

"So sweet," he murmured, cupping the thatch of silken hair with his hand. She moaned and pushed against his palm, breath puffing from her in ragged little gasps.

The sound of her hungry need for him made fire pool urgently in his body, swelling his already pulsing arousal against the warm curve of her buttocks until he could feel each thud of his heart.

Stacy's breath splintered into a low cry as Boyd slipped a long finger into her warmth, thrusting and retreating in a rhythm that tore at his control. Her back arched in a passionate reflex that pressed her hard against him.

He felt her shudder, then gasp and call his name. Unable to

hold back on the need clawing at him, he thrust forward slowly, teeth gritted against the urge to bury himself deep and fast. Instead, he made himself probe gently, rubbing with aching restraint against the hard little nub hidden between sleek, silken folds until he felt the tendons in his neck straining.

Stacy twisted sinuously, desperate to absorb more of the wild, sweet pleasure that was beyond ecstasy. The man she loved was filling her so completely, then slipping away before she tipped over the edge. She curled her fingers into the pillow, her breath coming in panting sobs of frustration and need.

"Is it good?" Boyd demanded, his voice a harsh rumble laced with strain.

"Yes, oh yes," she whispered, her voice as ragged as the edges of release just beyond her reach.

Boyd murmured her name on a groan as he unleashed a part of the savage need clawing at him. She was soft and yielding and hot, and he breathed a plea for patience into the damp, warm skin of her neck. One hand cupped her breast as he felt the tiny tremors tormenting him. The sound she made was as involuntary as the tightening of her body around him.

His own helpless cry was lost in the haze of the greatest pleasure he'd ever known.

Stacy woke with a smile on her face and a feeling of peace so complete she felt boneless. Enjoying a face-stretching yawn, she turned her head and cast a loving look on the naked man sprawled aggressively over a good two-thirds of the bed.

It was early, not yet six-thirty, and the sun streaming through the open window was gentle on his harsh, dark face. His whiskers were tawny against the darker skin, and his hair had grown longer, tossed by sleep into a wild tumble over his broad forehead. Soft and thick, it was a fascinating mixture of sand and silver with highlights of the same dark gold that formed his heavy eyebrows and thick eyelashes.

Tenderness filled her as she slowly extended a hand to trace the roguish cowlick above one temple. Though she was sure her touch was whisper light, he opened his eyes and looked at her with what she could only describe as a wary confusion in those grayer-than-gray eyes.

"Morning, sweetheart." She loved the gravel in his morning voice and the guarded smile that settled into his eyes.

"Good morning."

"How did you two ladies sleep?"

"So-so. I had my usual tussle with heartburn and Tory practiced *Swan Lake*." Smiling, she stretched a leg and arched her spine. She couldn't remember a time when her back didn't ache.

He flattened one large hand over her belly and cocked one eyebrow. "So your little girl has gone from placekicker to prima ballerina, huh?"

Stacy pressed her hand over his, enjoying the feeling of hard sinew and warm skin against hers, and nodded solemnly. "Much more feminine, don't you think?"

"Yeah, but not nearly as interesting."

"A matter of opinion, Dr. MacAuley."

A frown worked its way into his face, creasing his forehead and darkening his eyes. "Not doctor, not anymore."

She hesitated, then plunged ahead. "Fred Ivans doesn't think so."

Boyd lifted one eyebrow. "Fred? Since when have the two of you become so chummy?"

"Since I've taken four of his phone calls in the past two weeks. Phone calls which I might add you've yet to return."

Something dark and disturbing flickered in the depths of his eyes. "I've been busy helping Prudy fit cabinets made for a mansion into a space the size of a postage stamp."

Stacy smiled as she pictured Boyd and Prudy squabbling over angles and shims while sharing a beer in the midst of sawdust and random bits of lumber. Neither had let her lift a hand, except to drink the glass of milk they'd forced on her, but both had insisted that she give her unbiased opinion. No fool, she'd agreed with them both.

"I could call him back for you," she said as casually as an offer to iron a shirt. "Perhaps set up an appointment for the two of you to meet. Or better yet, why don't I invite him to dinner?''

He shook his head. ''You've got better things to do than entertain strangers.''

''But he's not a stranger to you.''

Even though he lifted a hand to play with a lock of her hair on the pillow, she could almost hear his protective walls clanging into place around his soul. ''Let it be, Stacy. I'm not going back into medicine. That part of my life is history.''

Keep it light, she told herself firmly. Don't push him too hard too fast. ''You're telling me you don't miss it?'' she chided with a grin.

''What's to miss?''

''The satisfaction of helping others?'' she suggested gently.

He snorted derisively. ''More like living with an exhaustion so thick even your eyelashes hurt and a stress level that would bring down an iron man.'' His voice was bland, his expression controlled as he propped himself on one elbow.

She let her smile fade. Instead of bantering now, they were sliding into an argument she'd sensed had to happen sooner or later. ''How about the thrill of relieving another person's pain?'' she murmured, her voice utterly serious and filled with a certainty that had grown stronger in the month she'd lived with him in the same house. ''Or maybe the joy of saving a life that would have surely ended if you hadn't been there?''

''It doesn't always work that way, Stacy. If you're too tired, under too much stress. Distracted.'' He shrugged, looked away. ''One wrong move and someone who should have lived dies.''

''But that didn't happen.''

''It might have. Could have.''

''You're afraid—''

''Yes, damn it,'' he all but shouted. ''I'm afraid. Now can we just leave it at that?'' He sat up quickly and left the bed to stalk out of the bedroom. An instant later she heard the bathroom door slam shut, followed shortly by the drone of the shower turned to full blast.

You can run from me but not yourself, my darling, she

thought sadly before getting herself, in stages, out of bed as well. She refused to feel guilty for nagging him in so good a cause. Not only for Boyd himself, but for the patients he would be able to treat.

Patients, she suspected, he would hover over the way he'd been hovering over her. Pampering her, bullying her, doing everything in his power to take care of her.

No, Boyd was meant to be a doctor. And if he weren't so darn stubborn, he'd admit it. To her and, more important, to himself.

After all, if he was so dead set against going back into medicine, why did he pore over the medical journals that came in the mail each month with the same intensity as a teenaged boy reading his first *Playboy*?

Because medicine is in his blood, she answered, slipping out of the skimpy nightgown that had been her birthday present to herself last year. Because he loves it, the same way I love teaching, she added, jerking open one of the two drawers in his bureau that held her clothes.

She dressed as quickly as her clumsy bulk would allow, then padded barefoot to the kitchen. The coffee was already brewed, thanks to the timer Boyd never failed to set as his last chore of the evening. As soon as she'd delivered the baby and stopped nursing, she intended to indulge in a veritable orgy of caffeine, she decided as she took her first greedy sip of her one and only cup.

A plaintive cry from outside cut through her satisfied sigh. Obviously Sunny was awake and ready to chow down. Grinning, Stacy grabbed another quick sip before putting down her mug to open the door under the sink.

"Greedy little freeloader," Stacy muttered as she scooped out a generous measure of dry food from the sack there. Twice since she'd found Sunshine on the doorstep, she'd had to buy more food. Boyd had scowled as she'd tossed a bag into their shopping cart, but so far, he hadn't uttered that first word about Sunny's future.

Sunshine was circling the deck with impatient little steps when Stacy threw open the door and called to her through the screen. With a gleeful look and a twitch of her gloriously fluffy tail, the yellow tabby trotted quickly to her bowl.

Stacy took a gingerly look to make sure her aggressive little huntress hadn't brought home yet another offering before opening the screen door. One morning she'd found a terrified mouse clutched between Sunny's sharp little claws. On another, a baby garter snake.

Stacy had managed to coax Sunny to release the mouse. The snake she'd left to Boyd, who'd grumbled and growled something about women being the death of a man, an ungracious comment that Stacy had generously assumed he'd been directing at Sunshine and not her.

"Today is shopping day, so I'll see if I can find you a nice little catnip mouse," she informed the kitten solemnly while filling the waiting bowl. And maybe a bed, she decided as she slowly straightened. Sleeping under the deck on an old towel was fine in summer, but Sunny would need a warmer spot in winter.

Watching Sunny dive into the food, she recalled the day shortly after Sunny's arrival when she'd come across Boyd backing out from under the deck. Checking the posts for rot, he'd told her before hustling her inside.

Acting on a hunch, she'd later found a moment to check those same posts and discovered the cozy little nest he'd made for the kitten next to the foundation's shelter.

A lump formed in her throat as she went inside to start breakfast. The man was maddeningly kindhearted and generous to everyone but himself. Was it any wonder she was head-over-heels crazy for the guy?

Drawing a ragged breath, she opened the door to the fridge and took out a carton of eggs. *Crazy* being the operative word, she reminded herself as she took a mixing bowl from the cupboard.

She couldn't begin to count the reasons why falling in love with Boyd MacAuley would be a disastrous mistake. So she hadn't bothered.

One by one she broke some eggs into the bowl. She would scramble them with ham, one of Boyd's favorites. To put him into a better mood, she told herself. Because on the way to the secondhand shop where she'd found a bassinet in fairly decent shape, she intended to tackle him about cleaning up the nursery.

In for a penny, in for a pound, she thought, beating the eggs furiously with a whisk.

"I'm sorry I was such a grouch." His voice came softly and close to her ear. Preoccupied with her own thoughts, she hadn't heard him come up behind her.

She dropped the whisk and turned to face him. He'd shaved, she noticed, and actually brushed his shower-damp hair into something resembling a definite style. "You've got to stop wearing that sexy after-shave," she teased before inhaling deeply.

"It's just soap," he said, parroting her words at the picnic.

When she laughed softly, he slid his arms around her swollen waist and pulled her closer until they were belly to belly.

"Can't be just soap," she responded, loving the feel of his arms around her.

"Word of honor," he said before leaning down to brush a kiss over her still parted lips. "But I'm glad you think it's sexy."

"Immensely," she murmured, giving in to the need to rest her head against his chest. Beneath the tight T-shirt she heard the steady thudding of his heart and wondered if he would miss her when she was on her own again.

She would miss him terribly, she admitted, closing her eyes and hugging him harder. "Are you sure you're feeling up to this expedition today?" he asked between the soft kisses he was pressing along her hairline.

"I'm fine," she murmured, all but purring as his hands stoked her spine in a lovely, soothing massage. "Besides, the man at Grandmother's Attic has only promised to hold the bassinet for me until noon today."

She felt a sigh run through him before he lifted his head. "Stacy, let me buy you a new bassinet. It'll be my gift to the baby."

"No, but you can paint this one for me. A soft pearly white I think."

His forehead creased into its familiar groove, which seemed deeper than usual. "Of course, I'll paint the blasted thing. But that's a damn pathetic present."

"Not to me."

He drew an impatient breath. "How about one of those changing things? The one with drawers and a padded top. Or a rocking chair? Every new mom needs a rocking chair."

With soft, welcoming cushions and a stool for her feet, she thought wistfully. "Someday, when I can afford it."

"Damn it, Stacy, you're being stubborn again. And for no good reason."

"Pregnant ladies don't have to have reasons," she murmured, glancing down at her belly. "That's one of the benefits of being an expectant mama."

He arched one eyebrow. "Ah, but one of the benefits of being an expectant mama's friend is the right to spoil said pregnant lady." He dropped a kiss on her nose before releasing her. "If you won't make a list of what you'll need, I'll just have to do it for you."

His grin was shaded toward cocky and his eyes glinted with so much mischief her heart turned over.

"Boyd, I don't even know where I'm going to live, or how much room I'm going to have there." She hesitated, then added, "I'm thinking about returning to Washington when the baby can travel."

Something changed in his eyes. "We'll work that out after you deliver."

She sighed, then turned to rest both hands on his shoulders. "Boyd, if it were just me, I'd be willing to take a chance on working anything out with you."

His grin came faster than usual and warmed her all the way to her toes. "Sounds promising. Why don't we start with this?" He cupped her shoulders in gentle hands and lowered his head to nuzzle her ear. She shivered and tried to resist the quick rush of pleasure.

"More?"

She made a sound that had him sliding his hands from her shoulders to the outer curves of her breasts. When he massaged them with his palms, she felt her breath stutter out in a soft moan.

"Come back to bed with me, honey."

"We have errands." Her protest sounded abysmally weak, and he chuckled.

"Later."

She melted against him, her pulse quickening. His mouth found hers a moment before the phone jangled. Boyd groaned and drew back. "Damn Alexander Graham Bell to hell," he grumbled before leaning past her to jerk the receiver from the hook.

"Yeah?" he demanded impatiently.

Her face still flushed and her heart still beating too fast, Stacy returned her attention to the half-beaten eggs while Boyd listened.

"Dr. Ivans, yes, sir, I did get your messages, and I appreciate—"

Stacy shot a glance over her shoulder and caught Boyd plowing stiff fingers through his hair. His gaze fastened on hers, and he scowled as he spoke into the receiver again. "Sir, I would hate to waste your time…no, it's not that, but—"

He closed his eyes on a wince, then braced his shoulders. "Yes, sir, I've got it. Tomorrow at twelve at the Mallory."

When Boyd hung up Stacy was smiling down at the eggs she'd whipped into a happy froth. She was so pleased she didn't even wince when he muttered a blistering oath.

# Fourteen

**B**uying the bassinet had been a mistake.

Sick at heart, Stacy stared down at the wicker she'd just scrubbed with disinfectant and strong soap, wondering how she could have been so insensitive. Why on earth hadn't she foreseen that the elderly proprietress of Grandmother's Attic would quite naturally assume that a man walking in with a waddlingly pregnant woman was the proud husband and father?

To his credit, Boyd had handled the sweet little old lady's beaming congratulations with a quiet dignity. While Stacy had counted out the money for the bassinet, he'd patiently listened to Mrs. Muldoon's effusive description of her own six pregnancies, followed by a detailed recitation of the ages and occupations of those six offspring, as well as numerous grandchildren.

*Is this your first?* Mrs. Muldoon had asked in all innocence as he'd prepared to carry away the bassinet.

On the drive home Stacy had apologized for putting him into such an awkward situation. In turn, he'd assured her that he'd enjoyed Mrs. Muldoon's rambling. Stacy had wanted to believe him. But the grim look around his eyes and the tension around his mouth told her that he was suffering.

They'd been silent as he'd carried the baby bed into the house and set it down in one corner of the living room. Silent, too, while he helped her put away the groceries they'd picked up on the way home. As soon as the last can was in the cupboard and the last carton of milk in the fridge, he'd changed into cutoff jeans and a tank top and gone outside to work in the yard.

To prune the hedge between his place and Prudy's, he'd said. The hedge that already marched drill-team straight from the sidewalk in front to the carport in the back. Running a finger over the nubby wicker, Stacy thought about her own experience with grieving—from the first tearing pangs of grief to a final acceptance of a reality she couldn't change, no matter how many tears she cried or how many prayers she prayed.

As though it were yesterday, she vividly recalled the awful anguish she'd felt the day she'd cleaned out Len's side of their bedroom closet. She'd cried over the ratty old bathrobe she'd hated and he'd loved, sobbed over the trophies and personal mementos he'd stashed on a top shelf. Packing the accumulation of his thirty years of living had symbolized the end of their life together. A final closure.

After the storage company's van had driven away, she'd sat in Len's chair at the kitchen table and cried until there'd been no more tears. Her life with the man she'd loved was over. Gone forever. Nothing would ever change that.

It was at that moment that she'd begun to heal, she realized now. When Len had returned with gasoline and rage to destroy the house, she'd been able to forgive him—and to forgive herself for being glad to be alive, even though, in all ways that mattered, he was dead.

Biting her lip, she turned slowly to look down the hall. The door at the end had been firmly closed since that first morning when she'd mistaken the nursery for Boyd's office. To her knowledge, Boyd never went in there. Certainly the layer of

dust she'd seen on the remnants of the furniture suggested that
the room had sat empty and abandoned for years.

Perhaps it was a good thing she hadn't broached the subject
of clearing away the debris this morning after all, she thought
as she walked resolutely toward the hall. Perhaps, if she made
a start, Boyd would feel more comfortable finishing. And in
the process, perhaps he'd find the sense of closure he needed.

Odds were he'd be upset with her, she reminded herself as
she opened the door to the nursery. He might even become
angry, in that steely, tight-lipped, tip-of-the-emotional iceberg
way she'd glimpsed at the Budget Motel when they'd been
discussing her toad of a landlord.

Anger she could handle, she told herself firmly, even if it
was directed at her. And forgive, because she understood the
depth of the pain and guilt fueling it. It was the image of him
living out his future embittered and alone that gave her the
courage to step into the hot, stuffy room where grief still hung
like a smothering pall of smoke.

Pressing a hand to the muscle in her back that had begun
aching while she scrubbed the bassinet, she stood in the middle
of the room and turned a slow, complete circle. She would
start in the middle and work toward the corners, she decided
with a heavy sigh. Good thing she'd had the foresight to buy
a box of extra-sturdy trash bags. As she retraced her steps to
the kitchen to fetch the box, she had a feeling she was going
to need every darn one.

"What in holy *hell* are you doing?"

Seated awkwardly in the middle of the floor she'd only half
cleared, Stacy was startled into gasping aloud, more because
of the barely restrained fury in Boyd's voice than its volume
which, in fact, was scarcely louder than a hiss.

Stiffening her aching back, she turned to look up at him.
The dangerous light in his dark eyes took her breath, and she
required a frozen moment to get it back.

"You need an office, and this room isn't being used," she
told him calmly when she could speak again.

"I have a corner of the living room, a desk and filing cabinet. That's all I need."

"You need *two* filing cabinets at the very least, and a table big enough to spread out blueprints. Provided you continue working as a contractor." She glanced down at the shards of bright yellow porcelain in her hands, the remains of what had once been a child's lamp with a smiling sun face. "If you go back into medicine, which is where you belong, you'll need a study."

She couldn't have imagined his eyes growing even more dangerous than they were, but the sudden chill slipping down her spine proved her wrong. "Back off, Stacy," he said slowly and distinctly. "I agreed to have lunch with Fred Ivans as a courtesy, nothing more."

"If you say so."

Boyd took a deep breath and tried to loop a knot around his unraveling temper. Get the hell out, he told himself. Walk it off before you do something you'll regret. But an impulse born in the dark and seething part of his soul prodded him to step into the room instead.

It wasn't anger driving him. That would be too easily vented.

No, it was the shock of being in this room again, with the memories waiting just beyond his field of vision to slam him bleeding and raw to the ground as they had before. And it was the look in Stacy's eyes that told him she understood exactly what he was feeling. Understood and was determined to help.

To care for him.

Nevertheless, anger was a part of it, the part that tore the hardest at his control. "When I said we'd work something out, I wasn't giving you permission to take over my house, or my life," he said, punching out each word in a low, flat tone that seemed to echo inside his head.

The hurt that flashed into her eyes tore even more savagely at him. But once said, the words couldn't be recalled.

"Isn't that exactly what you did a month ago? Take over *my* life?" Stacy tossed the bits of broken glass into the nearest trash bag with such force they shattered.

"Don't be ridiculous."

"Ridiculous? Hah! What I'm being is honest. The old double standard is alive and well on this end of Mill Works Ridge. Practiced with great skill by the great Boyd MacAuley, a man who's so busy feeling sorry for himself he can't see just how blessed he is."

Boyd glowered down at her, his eyes the color of ice over flint, his skin bleached white along the hard line of his mouth. "Go ahead, get it all out," he said, barely moving his lips.

"You think it's perfectly okay to come marching into my motel room and scoop me up against my will, okay to concoct some kind of thinly disguised story about needing clerical help as an excuse to give me money."

Stacy jerked in air and felt a tug in her belly. "And then, to top it off, make me fall in love with you when I know perfectly well how stupid that would be."

Color flooded Boyd's face, turning it dark. But it was the flash of pain in his eyes that had her heart tearing. A man in love feels joy when his love is returned—not anguish. "But that's my problem, not yours," she went on, determined to say it all. "Just about everyone who knows you wants to help you get past the tragedy you suffered. And it is a tragedy, Boyd. All I had to do was look around in here to see how well loved that little girl of yours was."

His mouth jerked, and Stacy felt tears welling in her eyes. "But you won't let anyone close enough to help. You talk to me about pride, and yet you've got yours wrapped around you so tight I'm surprised it hasn't strangled you long before now."

"Pride, hell! Just because I don't go crying to my friends when I'm feeling blue doesn't make me the kind of jerk you've just described."

Stacy looked around her in a slow, meaningful way before returning her gaze to his. "A man who would live with this for three years isn't just feeling blue, Boyd. Surely you can see that." She bit her lip, lifted her chin. Met his gaze. "You need help. Professional help."

She held her breath and prayed to see hope replace the icy

distance in his eyes. Instead they suddenly looked terribly tired. "I've had professional help. A padded room, a strait-jacket. Hell, I did it all."

Stacy felt her jaw drop, and her skin chill. "What?"

"I cracked up, Stacy. Split wide open. Ended up in a county mental hospital down near Roseburg." He glanced away, his jaw taut.

"But when...why?"

When his gaze came back to hers again, he looked resigned. "The when and the why are the same. I committed myself right after I looked down at the patient whose belly I'd just opened and saw my wife looking back at me. My wife who'd been dead for months." He bit off a harsh laugh. "I even heard her voice, clear as a bell, begging me to cut her open at the side of the road that night and take the baby."

Stacy blinked, scarcely able to wrap her mind around the enormity of what he'd just told her. "Prudy said you'd gone away," she said quietly, crowded by a regret she knew would be with her for the rest of her life.

"I went to visit my sister Marty in Roseburg. I made it as far as her front porch sometime in the middle of the night. She found me sitting there the next morning, staring at nothing. Or so she said. I don't remember."

Stacy heard only a flat declaration of fact in his tone, but she sensed the effort he was making to tell her even a fraction of what he must have gone through. What she'd seen Len go through.

"You must have gotten help. In the hospital."

One side of his mouth slanted. "Oh yeah, I got help. A nice heavy slug of Thorazine every four hours."

She drew a careful breath. "Not all psychiatrists are drug happy. In fact, I know a woman in Washington—"

"You're fighting after the bell, Stacy. I threw in the towel years ago."

Before she could find the words to plead, he turned and left her sitting exactly where he'd found her. In the ruins of his life. And of her dreams.

* * *

Scowling down at the cat meowing plaintively around her feet, Prudy rapped an impatient tattoo on Boyd's back door. It had been almost three hours since he'd nearly broadsided her and her Volvo at the entrance to their driveway. He hadn't so much as glanced her way as he gunned his truck into traffic. If Stacy had been with him, Prudy might have assumed he'd been tearing off to the hospital, but he'd been alone.

Because the plumbing contractor and his helper had been waiting on her doorstep when she'd pulled into the carport, she hadn't stopped by to check on Stacy immediately. "Damn it, I shouldn't have waited," she muttered to the kitten before lifting her fist to knock again.

Before her knuckles made contact, however, she heard the bolt turning.

"Are you all right?" she demanded the moment Stacy had the door open.

"Definitely not," Stacy muttered, stepping back with what Prudy gauged to be considerable effort.

"You're in labor?"

Stacy's tired grin twisted into a grimace. "Oh yes."

After an initial flare of anxiety, Prudy felt her emotions settle. "How far apart are the contractions?"

"Seven minutes last time I checked."

Prudy glanced at her watch before slipping an arm around Stacy's waist. "Come on, let's get you into a nice comfortable chair."

"I'm not ready for this. I am really not ready."

Prudy heard the rising note of panic in Stacy's voice and fought down a grin. "Have you phoned Jarrod?"

"His service. He's in the delivery room."

Prudy nodded. "Once I get you settled, I'll get through to him for you."

Stacy felt another cramp begin in the middle of her back and finger inch by inch toward her belly where it twisted into an agonizing knot. "Breathe into it," she heard Prudy murmur, and tried to comply. But her concentration kept fragmenting. "I wish Boyd were here," she muttered when at last the contraction eased off.

Prudy helped her into the corner of the sofa, then knelt next to her to take her pulse. "Where is the big lug anyway?" Prudy asked when she was finishing counting.

"Running."

"Come again?"

"We had a fight." Stacy let out a puff of air. She was scared and tired and worried sick. "Oh Prudy, I blew it big-time."

"I doubt that, Stace."

Stacy rested her head against the cushion and closed her eyes. After the first few contractions, the baby had stopped moving. Preparing herself, Stacy prayed. "He's given me so much." Everything but the one thing she prized above all. The one thing he didn't have in him to give. "I wanted to give him something in return. I thought, if I cleaned away the mess in the nursery, it might…oh, no, not another one!" The contraction lasted longer and bit deeper, leaving Stacy panting and damp from the sweat that had oozed from her pores.

"Five minutes," Prudy murmured before getting to her feet. "Try to relax. I'm going to track down Jarrod and tell him we're on our way."

Stacy pressed her hands to her belly and slumped against the cushions. In her dreams she'd envisioned Boyd sitting next to her at this moment, holding her hand, talking to her in that calm, raspy voice that had quieted her fears after the accident.

"Oh, Boyd, I really made a mess of things, didn't I?"

Her only answer was the hard thudding of her heart over the baby whose face she was about to see for the first time.


Boyd had come home prepared to make peace, only to find a note from Prudy taped to the back door, telling him that Stacy was in labor and on her way to the hospital.

*P.S. I fed the cat,* he read before adding an obscene postscript of his own.

Two minutes later he was back on the road, the acid of fear burning a hole in his gut. Because he wanted to jam the accelerator to the floor, traffic signals, other motorists and cops be damned, he made himself drive with extra care. According to the time Prudy had jotted under her signature, they'd been gone from the house for over four hours. Four hours when he should have been with Stacy, keeping the promise he'd made her instead of skulking like a wounded animal in a smoky bar, trying to convince himself to get blind, stinking drunk.

When he'd left the place as sober as he'd been when he entered, he'd settled only one thing in his mind—he had no right to jump down Stacy's throat for trying to drag him kicking and screaming out of the cold and into the sunshine.

The sunshine she could create with just a smile.

Sunshine he'd done his best to drown in self-pity.

The lights outlining the hospital parking lot were winking on when he pulled into the closest slot. Twisting the key so hard it nearly snapped before he jerked it from the ignition, he was out of the car and heading for the entrance at a dead run before the engine had time to stop.

Stacy woke to a shaft of sunshine slanting across her bed and a room filled with flowers. Before her delighted smile reached full bloom, however, it froze at the sight of Boyd sprawled in a chair pulled close to the bed, sound asleep.

Still dressed in the tank top and shorts he'd worn for gardening, he needed a shave, a shower and, from the stamp of exhaustion on his abnormally pale face, a good night's sleep. But it was the soft white teddy bear still crooked in the corner of one arm that brought tears to her eyes.

Biting her lip, she reached out to touch the strong hand cupped protectively around the bear's tiny foot. It was only the faintest of touches, a tactile whisper, but it was enough to jerk him awake.

For an instant his eyes were filled with anguish before they turned dark. "You look...beautiful," he said, his voice thick. "But I miss your round tummy."

Stacy felt a blush stealing over her cheeks as she glanced down at the flat expanse of white hospital sheet stretching from her breasts to her toes. Which she wiggled, just because she could now see them move. "I don't," she murmured with fervent relief.

Even as he managed a smile, he felt his heart tumbling in

his chest. She was beyond lovely, with the sun kissing gold into her hair and the joy of motherhood shining from her eyes. The lips that he'd kissed with such passion were sweetly curving, inviting his. All that lingered of the idealistic young man he'd once been yearned to take her into his arms with a pledge of forever.

"The flowers are beautiful," she said, glancing around. "Are they from you?"

"No, from Mrs. Matsuka."

"Who?"

He loved the way her eyebrows swooped together and her mouth pouted when she was puzzled. "Mary Matsuka, downstairs. In the florist shop."

Her laugh trilled softly. "You must have cleaned her out."

"Not quite. She had this ugly cactus thing that I rejected."

She laughed again, before thanking him.

Boyd sat up, his stiff muscles protesting the sudden demand, and tried to level his emotions. Arriving at the maternity wing to find that Stacy had already delivered had only added barbs to the guilt already damn near choking him like a hangman's noose. Jarrod's repeated assurances that both she and the baby were fine had only paid out a little slack.

"Stacy, I—"

"Don't say it," she ordered fiercely, knitting her brows. "It's not your fault I went into labor, and it's not your fault I delivered so fast you weren't here to hold my hand." She took a breath, then curved her lips into an angel's smile. "But I have to admit I wish you could have seen her when she was born."

Something thick clogged Boyd's throat. "So do I," he said gruffly. "But I did see her when she was only a little more than an hour old. And yes, Mom, she is hands down the prettiest baby in the nursery."

The laconic hint of humor in his tone had her laughing softly. "Ouch," she muttered when a twinge of pain brought her up short. "I swear, the worst part of having a baby is the episiotomy."

He looked so uncomfortable at that she had to grin.

"Uh, Jarrod said you had an easy delivery."

"Hah!" Stacy pressed the button to raise the head of the bed and wondered when they were going to bring Tory in to nurse for the first time.

"And that for such a ladylike woman you displayed a remarkable grasp of the, uh, more colorful phrases of the English language."

Swore like a cowhand on the losing end of a tussle with a mean-ass bull is what Jarrod had really said. Boyd had nearly decked him until he'd assured him Stacy had sailed through her delivery with no complications. But, now, as he surreptitiously studied her pale face and too bright eyes, he wondered if Jarrod had taken one look at the sorry shape he'd been in last night and shaded the truth.

He was about to run through a comprehensive list of diagnostic questions when a nurse he didn't know walked in pushing a bassinet on wheels. "Good morning," she chirped to them both.

"Good morning," Stacy replied, her face alight with anticipation as the nurse expertly scooped the swaddled baby from the plastic shell.

"Didn't hear a peep out of her all night," she said, settling the baby in Stacy's arms. "Best little munchkin in the nursery." As though offering him the credit, the nurse gave him a smile that he couldn't quite return.

"Oh Boyd, she's even more wonderful than I remembered." The awe in Stacy's voice had him shoring up walls. When she brought her gaze to his, he saw tears glistening in her eyes.

"As wonderful as her mom," he said, before he realized he should have cleared his throat of the thickness there first.

Her suddenly trembling smile told him she understood. And forgave.

"Has your milk let down yet?" the nurse asked, drawing Stacy's gaze from his.

"Not yet." She fumbled with the snaps at the shoulder. When she had trouble, the nurse helped, careful to keep Stacy's breast covered.

"Sometimes it takes the stimulation of the baby's mouth." The nurse cast a sidelong glance toward Boyd, before asking Stacy brightly, "Is there anything else I can do for you?"

"Nothing, thanks."

"When you're finished nursing, ring the desk."

Stacy nodded. "But Tory stays in here with me, right?"

The nurse smiled. "Yes, she stays with you. No one would dare try to take her away." After giving Stacy an encouraging pat on the shoulder, the nurse left the three of them alone.

Stacy glanced down at the small, red face of her daughter and, for a moment, couldn't breathe. From a moment of frenzied desperation had come a perfect little soul. A new life. A child with Len's dramatic coloring and her features replicated in miniature.

Sweet Victoria.

Love rushed through her, filling her, warming her. Lifting her head, she looked over at Boyd and smiled. "I knew I loved her, but I had no idea how deeply until this moment."

Boyd drew a breath. It was time for him to leave.

He shifted, sat up, balanced the stuffed bear he'd forgotten he had between his rough hands. Looked down at the floor, then lifted his gaze to hers, only to find her watching him with eyes softened by an understanding that hurt him to accept.

"It's over, isn't it?" she said gently. "Our time together."

He didn't know what to say, so he simply looked at her.

"You keep telling me not to thank you, so I won't. But you have to know what…how much you mean to me. How much you'll always mean to me."

His breath jammed in his throat, Boyd laid the bear on the mattress next to Stacy's hip and got to his feet. It hurt to see the hope shimmering in her eyes as she watched him.

"Would you like to hold her before you go?"

Boyd felt an ache. "I'm too raunchy," he said, glancing down at his sweat-stained shirt.

"Not for us."

He saw the hope die in her eyes, and wanted to crawl. "Promise me you'll stay in my house until you're on your feet again," he said, his voice strained.

"All right." Because he'd expected her to protest, her easy acquiescence all but broke his heart.

"I'll leave a check for you on the kitchen table. I want you to cash it and use the money for a new start. When you're solvent again, you can pay me back." Before the militant light in her eyes could find voice, he lifted a hand to add, "You can even pay me interest if that makes you feel better."

"Oh, Boyd," she whispered, breaking his heart.

"I won't be there when you return so I'll say goodbye now."

"Where...where are you going?"

Because he didn't know, he merely shrugged. "Take care of yourself and Victoria." As he'd done once before, he leaned down to brush a kiss across her lips.

"Boyd, please—" He touched a finger to her lips, stemming the words he knew she would regret.

"It's better this way, Stacy." He hesitated, then, because he couldn't help himself, he leaned down to kiss the baby's rose-petal cheek and, for an instant, thought of his own little angel. Pain slammed into him with such force he nearly cried out in a plea for mercy. Instead, he made himself straighten, made himself smile. Made himself walk away.

# Fifteen

At the sound of footsteps approaching the small, pine-paneled office, Boyd turned away from the window where he'd been watching a hummingbird darting in and out of the honeysuckle bushes. He'd been thinking of Stacy, of course. Wondering if she were well. And happy.

Dr. Skip Weilbren came into the office with the same harried look Boyd remembered on that terrible day ten weeks ago when he'd shown up here to ask a favor of his old buddy from med school. Checking himself into a psychiatric hospital hadn't been the easiest thing Boyd had ever done, but those first few minutes with Skip had gone a long way toward convincing him he was doing the right thing.

"Well, Boyd, I can't say it's been fun, but it's sure been interesting."

Boyd heard the humor threaded through Skip's Kansas twang and grinned. "It's been pure hell, and you know it."

"Yeah, well you know us farm boys. We like a hard nut to crack now and then."

Boyd groaned at the bad pun, winning him one of Skip's triumphant chuckles. "Gotcha again."

"Bastard."

For a moment, the years seemed to fall away, and they grinned at each other like wild and woolly college boys who'd just pulled a prank on the dean. Then Skip thrust out his hand and Boyd took it. "You did good, my friend." Skip's voice was suddenly serious, his eyes conveying messages he didn't seem able to put into words.

Boyd could sympathize. There was a lump in his own throat the size of a golf ball. "Thanks for hanging in there with me," he said gruffly.

Skip nodded. "You didn't really need to be here, you know. Sooner or later, you would have worked all this out for yourself."

"Maybe."

"True story. I just shoved you in the right direction now and then."

"Kicked my sorry ass was more like it." Boyd swallowed hard, and noticed that Skip did too.

"Well, I guess I'd better get out of your hair—what little there is left of it."

Skip swiped his palm over a scalp as bald as a grape and scowled. "I notice you're leaving here with a little more gray than you brought with you, old son."

"Trick of the light." Boyd reached down for his old duffle bag, the only luggage he'd brought with him.

"Still planning to take Ivans up on his offer?"

"If he'll have me, yeah."

"And Stacy? Have you called her?" Skip asked suddenly, perceptive as always.

"No." Boyd slung the bag over his shoulder. Then he met his friend's gaze. "I'm not sure I'm ready for a wife and kids yet. Until I'm damned sure, I just don't feel like it's right to clutter up her life. You know what I mean?"

Skip nodded. "Just don't wait too long, Boyd. Remember what's brought you this far, hmm?"

Boyd forced a smile. "Yeah. 'Don't think it to death, just do it.'"

"It's normal to feel a little hesitant, you know."

Boyd arched an eyebrow. "Hesitant? Try scared spitless."

* * *

Stacy was determined to leave Boyd's home shining and bright. In two days she was to move into the two bedroom duplex she'd found within walking distance of Lewis and Clark Elementary School where she was now happily teaching morning kindergarten on a permanent basis.

Because she had very little to take with her, she'd decided to clean first and then pack right before she left. She started with the kitchen and had finished all but the oven by the time she put Tory down for her afternoon nap.

"There you go, my little pink dumpling," she crooned as she snuggled Tory into the bassinet that was soon to be replaced by the new crib Stacy had ordered. If all went well, it would be delivered to the duplex on moving day.

Stacy's soft crooning seemed to amuse Tory, and she chortled happily, kicking off the light cover her mother had just tucked in so carefully around her.

"Hey, enough of that," Stacy reprimanded in a lilting tone. "Summer's over. I don't want you catching cold right before you start day care."

Stacy burrowed her face into the baby's tummy, and Tory squealed her delight. Laughing softly, Stacy made little biting movements while Tory's tiny fingers pulled at her hair. By the time they'd finished their ritual pre-nap play, Tory had destroyed the neat bun on the top of Stacy's head. After making sure no pins had dropped into the bassinet, Stacy headed to the bathroom to repair the damage, only to be distracted by the shrill pealing of the doorbell.

Since only delivery men and religious zealots came to the front door, she was frowning when she pulled it open.

"Boyd!" Her hand flew to her mouth in surprise and her heart started beating wildly.

"Hi, Stacy. I hope this isn't a bad time to stop by."

"I…we were just playing. Tory and me. Us." She realized she was babbling and shut her mouth with a snap.

"Sounds like fun."

He looked wonderful, she decided. Rested and tanned and younger somehow. Even his jeans seemed new, and enticingly snug. Beneath a burgundy University of Kansas sweatshirt his chest seemed wider than she remembered. As she returned her gaze to his, she also noticed that he seemed tense. An awful, brittle kind of tension that had every muscle in his body knotted.

"You've gained weight," she blurted. "I mean, it looks good on you."

His eyes crinkled in a smile that didn't quite reach his mouth. "I've been working out."

"Good." Her voice scratched, and she swallowed. "Uh, would you like to come in?" she asked politely and then laughed. "That's a silly question. It's your house, after all."

She stepped back, acutely aware that her hair was hanging in clumps and her ratty old T-shirt had a smear of baby beets on one shoulder where Tory had spit up on her.

"How's the baby?" he asked when she'd closed the door and turned to face him. He'd brought the autumn smells in with him—wind and wood smoke and a hint of the storm that was brewing.

"Tory's blooming, as fat as a little Buddha. Would you like to see her? I just put her down for a nap, but—"

He raked a hand through his hair, then glanced around. Almost as if he were searching for something. Words, maybe? When he swung his gaze back to her, he shifted his weight from one powerfully muscled leg to the other. His eyes had a shuttered look, as if heavy curtains had been drawn over his emotions. "Maybe later."

The excitement that had started to kindle in her withered and died. "I can offer you coffee or a soft drink."

"Nothing, thanks." One side of his mouth kicked up, his version of a smile. "I notice you didn't mention herbal tea."

She made a face. "I convinced Luke to let me switch to decaf coffee."

His eyes narrowed ever so slightly. "Jarrod always was a patsy for a pretty woman."

Pretty? Is that what he thought of her? Stacy felt her hopes stirring in the ashes where she'd consigned them, only to haul herself up short. She hadn't heard a word from this man in three months. He was just being kind, that was all. Acting like a gentleman, as always.

"Would you like to sit down?" she asked, gesturing toward the sofa where he'd once slept.

His gaze made another fast journey around the room before

settling on her face again. He was acting as if he were a stranger who'd just stepped into a strange house. And yet, there was something vibrant and strong about him now that hadn't been there the last time she'd seen him.

"Sure I'm not keeping you from something?"

"Actually you are. I was just about to clean the oven, so I'd appreciate it if you'd sit and give me an excuse to play hostess."

Boyd drew the first deep breath he'd been able to manage since he'd walked up the front walk. At least she hadn't kicked him out on his butt.

"Ladies first," he insisted. His grandmother would be proud of him for remembering his manners when damn near every nerve ending in his body was screaming at him to take her in his arms and kiss her senseless.

Instead of sitting next to him as he'd hoped, she chose the wing chair opposite, settling into the elegant cushions with a sensuous grace that sent his hormones racing.

"You're thin," he said, eyeing the sloppy shirt that had once draped over her belly with very little room to spare.

"Thinner anyway," she said, laughing. "I still have five more baby pounds to lose."

"I think you look fine just the way you are." In reality, he thought she looked like an angel. The same angel who'd haunted his dreams night after night for longer than he cared to remember.

Stacy drew a shaky breath. Now what? she wondered desperately "Did you enjoy your...vacation?"

"Not particularly, but it was necessary."

"You needed to get away." It wasn't a question.

"Yes. Just as I needed to come back."

"Loose ends," she murmured, conscious of his attention to detail.

"Something like that."

Stacy forced a smile. "You'll be happy to hear this particular *end* is no longer loose," she said with another quick little laugh. "Tory and I are moving to our own place the day after tomorrow, so your timing is darn near perfect." Before he could reply, she hurried on. "And you'll also be happy to know that I'm gainfully employed, financially comfortable, and in the very best of health."

"I can see that." Boyd realized his hands were sweating and wiped them on this thighs. "Am I allowed to ask how you accomplished all of this in such a short time?"

A shadow drifted across her face and he tensed. "The employment came as a result of the applications I put in before the end of the school year—with a little help from Mrs. Marsh."

"Mrs. Marsh?"

"The principal of Lewis and Clark Elementary. Remember that day in the ER when I asked someone to give her a call?" Without waiting for his response, she added softly, "The money came from Len, indirectly. Survivor's benefits. I'd actually forgotten the policy even existed, and then when I called Len's parents to tell them about Tory, they told me the insurance company had been looking for me."

She wasn't rich by any means, but she had enough now to repay Boyd and settle her hospital bills, with plenty left over to let her get by with teaching only part-time while Tory was tiny.

He nodded. "I think that in some part of his mind he was still the man you married. The man who loved you. It might help you to remember that."

"Yes," she murmured softly, glancing at the photo of Victoria on the small table by the window. "I've promised myself Tory will know only about the loving side of her daddy." Len was there, she thought. In the sparkle of the baby's eyes and in her jet curls. But so was Boyd, although his blood would never flow in Tory's veins.

"I named her Victoria MacAuley Patterson." Afraid to look at him, she directed her shaky smile at the baby's photo instead. "I hope you don't mind."

The sudden silence was thick enough to smother dreams. Squaring her shoulders, she shifted her gaze, made herself face him. Utterly still, he was staring at her, his forehead creased in that same familiar line.

"I can always change it, you know. If you'd rather. It was just a whim, a...spur-of-the-moment thing. Postnatal hormones, I guess."

He nodded slowly and she noticed he was rubbing his hands back and forth on his thighs again. To keep from strangling her? "And certainly there's no obligation on your part. None whatsoever. I don't want you to ever feel that there is. You've done so much for us already that I don't know how to express my gratitude. Words alone just don't seem enough, and—"

She saw his big chest heave and his shoulders brace. "Stacy, I—"

"There you go again," she cried, leaping to her feet. "Telling me not to thank you."

"Is that what I'm doing?"

"In your way, yes!" Close to tears, she tried to pull righteous indignation around her like a shield. Instead, she only succeeded in making herself feel more exposed. "It isn't just about money, Boyd, and my paying you back with interest. Can't you understand that?"

"Stacy, I—"

She threw up her hand. "Just listen. For once. Just listen to me. Okay?" She hugged her waist, took a fast turn past the stereo, then came back around to face him. "At one of the worst times in my life, you were there for me. A total stranger, and you gave me a hand up when no one else would. But, even more importantly, you gave me the time, and the space I needed, and the support to get my confidence back. How can I put a dollar value on that?"

He parted his lips as if to speak. She cut him off with another wave of her hand.

"The answer is, I can't. Never, not in a million years. All I can do is say thank you. But every time I try, you won't listen. And, let me tell you, I'm getting very tired of it."

He just sat there, staring at her, his expression rather dazed. Stacy took that as a good sign. At least he wasn't cutting her off this time, pretending that what he'd done for her was next to nothing.

A painful crushing sensation entered her chest. Seemingly from out of nowhere, another stream of words backed up in her throat. Without consciously making the decision, she blurted them out. "If you want to deny you have any feelings, that's fine. We all have to deal with things in our own way, and I understand that. But don't deprive me of the right to express mine, or tell me they're silly or not real when I do try to express them.''

"Stacy, I never meant to do that," he interrupted. "Your feelings matter very much to me. I don't think they're silly, or that they aren't real. If I said or did anything that—''

"If you said or did anything?" she countered incredulously. "When I told you I loved you, you said I didn't. As if I'm a child who doesn't know her own mind. Well, let me tell you something. I'm *not* a child. I think I know what I'm feeling and what I'm not, and I'd appreciate it if you wouldn't tell me differently.''

He rose, but he didn't come to her. Didn't take her into his arms and say the words she'd always made him say in her daydreams. "I remember my grandmother telling me a gentleman never contradicted a lady—even if she was dead wrong.''

Stacy blinked. Then frowned. "I'm not wrong," she said in a strained, twangy voice. "There, you see? You're doing it again. Telling me—''

"Actually, in this instance, *you're* telling *me*." He took one step, then stopped as though changing his mind about approaching her. "At the risk of setting you off again, let me say that I wasn't going to *tell* you anything. I was going to ask you.''

"Ask me what?''

"Ask you if you'd consider changing Victoria's name—''

"I've already said it was just a whim," she assured him. "A foolish fancy." For good measure she waved her hand again to show it meant nothing to her. Nothing at all.

Boyd waited until he was sure she was finished reassuring him. When she said nothing more, he took another cautious step toward her. He could smell her scent, a combination of baby powder, cleaning soap and woman.

"Nothing about you is foolish, or silly," he said when she locked her gaze on his. "And I happen to like your whims.''

"You do?''

He saw something leap into her eyes and felt the iron band around his chest ease off a notch. "In fact, on the way here I got to thinking it was a great day for a picnic.''

She looked confused. "But it's going to pour down rain any second now."

"Is it? Funny, I can only see sunshine."

Stacy realized she was having trouble breathing. When he came closer, she stopped breathing at all. He didn't touch her, yet his gaze seemed to pour over her, warming her as surely as a caress.

"Someday, when things calm down, I want to tell you where I've been, what I've been doing," he said, his voice husky.

"Someday I'd like to hear it," she said.

"I, uh, was asking you a question, remember?"

She'd forgotten, but nodded anyway. And then remembered. "About the baby's name."

"Yes. Well, I'm honored, of course." He paused to swipe his hand through the glossy thickness of his hair again. "But I was wondering…hoping that you might consider changing her name to Victoria Patterson MacAuley."

Stacy opened her mouth, then shut it. And opened it again when he grinned. "Now that's a first, my Stacy struck speechless."

He lifted a hand and eased a lock of hair away from her cheek. "I've missed you, honey. Not only in my bed, but in my life."

"I've missed you, too," she whispered. "Every time I nurse Tory, I think of you." It took her a second to realize what she'd said. And that he could take her words to mean more than she'd intended. "That is—"

He silenced her by putting two fingers against her lips. "Shh. Let me get this out while I can, though God knows, if I don't kiss you soon, I'm going to explode."

Stacy felt happiness burst inside her, but she managed to keep her expression calm. "We certainly can't have that."

Boyd took a deep breath, noticed that wasn't enough, and took another. "I'm no prize, I realize that. I come with a lot of extra baggage I'm trying to work loose, and I have no idea what kind of a future I can make for us." He grabbed more air, then went on. "But I figure between the two of us we can make a go of things."

Suddenly Stacy was scared. "Because you think we would make a good team?" she asked softly.

"A great team," he said, and her heart sank.

"And good parents?"

"The best—at least one of us." She saw the pulse hammering in his tanned throat and wondered about it.

"And lovers?" Her voice slid lower and lingered.

A flame leapt in his eyes. "I'm counting on that."

There was one question left, one she couldn't bring herself to ask. As though he'd heard her thoughts, he dropped his hand to her shoulder. "Is that it? Can I kiss you now?"

"Not yet."

"No?"

"No. I have a question for you." If she had the nerve to get out the words.

"Okay, but I warn you I'm not much good at explaining myself."

Stacy swallowed the lump in her throat. Fear, she thought. Or maybe anticipation. "Did you just ask me to marry you?" She was hedging, but then, she'd never been known for her bravery.

His eyebrows swooped together. "I thought that was pretty clear." He sighed. "I guess I forgot women need the words."

"This woman, anyway," Stacy muttered.

"Okay, here goes. Stacy Patterson, will you marry me?"

Instead of answering, she merely looked up at him with those beautiful golden eyes that seemed to pull him in and arouse him at the same time. "And have my children? Five or six, I think Madame said."

She smiled at that, and he started to relax—until he realized she hadn't answered. He felt an icy panic uncoiling in his belly and cursed himself for an idealistic idiot. So she'd said she loved him. Big deal.

"Damn it, Stacy, you have to marry me."

That got her attention. "I do? Why?"

"Because you make me laugh. Because you make me want to live instead of merely exist. Because I'm empty without you." He drew in a deep breath and took the biggest chance of his life. "And because I love you."

With a little cry she launched herself at him, and he caught her. Around and around he swung her, his lips on hers, and his heart in her small, clever hands.

When the kiss ended, Stacy was crying and laughing, and his eyes were suspiciously bright. "In case you haven't figured it out yet, I just accepted your proposal."

Boyd looked down into Stacy's shimmering eyes and felt the tension that always rode him easing away. He was whole again, free of the black nightmares. He would never be alone again, not with this woman standing beside him.

He cleared his throat and smiled down at her, knowing with a rock-solid certainty that she would hold his happiness in her heart for the rest of his natural life. And maybe even longer. Some things ran so deep and were so much a part of the sunlight that even death couldn't extinguish them. He had a feeling the love he felt for her was one of those things.

"If you're finally done harassing me, I think I'd like to see my daughter now."

Stacy heard the love aching in his voice and blinked back tears. She'd let him go, and by some miracle, he'd come back to her. It was almost too wonderful to be real, and yet, in another part of her heart, she knew it couldn't have happened any other way. His past had stolen him from her for a brief time, but his future had brought him full circle, right back into her arms. Because this was where he belonged.

"We've just been waiting for you to ask."

\* \* \* \* \*

*Turn the page for a sneak preview of*
*MOMMY BY SURPRISE, Paula Detmer Riggs's exciting*
*second book in the* MATERNITY ROW *series.*
*Coming in July 1997, only from*
*Silhouette Intimate Moments.*

# Mommy By Surprise

All eyes turned toward the sound of a heavy door banging shut as Case came striding out of the gloom at the rear of the church, still tugging on a suit jacket over the wide expanse of white shirt molding his impressive chest. He moved like a man with a mission, his walk part swagger, part power, the muscles bunching in his thighs with each step he took, drawing the sharply creased cloth of his trouser legs taut.

Watching him with hungry eyes, Prudy remembered the last time she'd seen him naked. How tempted she'd been to run her fingers through the softly curling chest hair. How fast her heart had beaten when she'd realized the strength he'd been hiding beneath the conservative clothing of a civilized man.

A part of her ached to feel that hard chest pressed against her breasts, while his arms tightened around her and his mouth came crashing down for a hard possessive kiss.

"Uncle Case!" Molly's smile was rainbow bright. As bright as Prudy's own had once been at the sight of her handsome husband charging through the door, his arms already reaching for her.

Prudy sucked in a breath, and waited for the moment she'd

dreaded for weeks to be over and done with. To get through this baptism, at which she and Case were standing up as godparents, with some semblance of control was all she wanted. If she could retain at least some of her pride and dignity while she was at it, that would be nice, as well. Surviving this was the main thing on her agenda, though.

"It'll be okay," she whispered to the baby in her arms, who didn't stir. In spite of his inner toughness and sometimes blunt manner, Case was a gentleman at heart. No matter what kind of resentment he might still harbor against his ex-wife, he wouldn't let that bleed over onto a sacred ceremony. His sense of propriety and decency was nearly as strong as his will.

Still, she couldn't prevent the sudden fluttering in the pit of her stomach—like hundreds of feather dusters all waving at once. It was the same feeling Case had aroused in her the first time they'd met. She'd been just a few years older than Molly, a brand-new RN who'd moved to Portland to take a job at Portland General. Case had been twenty-seven and gorgeous in his cop's uniform, with a body honed to a lean toughness by the physical work he'd done to put himself through college and a wickedly sensual gleam in his midnight blue eyes.

He'd gotten himself cut up on a fence while chasing a fourteen-year-old kid who'd stolen a souped-up Camaro, then, like a jackass, rear-ended Case's patrol car while pretending he could drive.

Determined to be big-city blasé instead of small-town awed, Prudy had ordered Patrolman Randolph around like a drill sergeant, then giggled when the big tough cop had displayed an endearing terror of needles. She'd fallen in love between the first and second sutures the trauma doctor had stitched into Case's injured shoulder.

"Sorry, little bit," Case said to Molly now as he reached the front of the church. "I had trouble getting away." He leaned closer to kiss his niece's cheek, and sunlight caught the inky silk of his hair, finding traces of silver among the thick strands. Though he'd always worn his hair longer than fashion dictated, it was now long enough to fall past his shoulders without the restraint of the rubber band pulling it back into a ponytail. No doubt about it, Prudy thought with a sad pang, her ex-husband was still a seductively attractive—and intimidating—man.

Molly introduced her uncle to the minister, who lifted his snowy eyebrows at the mention of Case's last name. "Oh, then you and this lovely lady are married?" the pastor said, beaming paternally from one to the other.

"Not anymore," Prudy informed him, finally finding her smile as she met Case's gaze. His eyes were still the color of midnight, with smudges of obsidian around the irises. Predatory eyes, she'd once called them, until they warmed with an inner fire. And then she'd lost the ability to form a coherent thought.

Seasoned by time, his face was ruggedly hewn, more angles than curves, with a lack of symmetry she'd always found irresistible, even as it hinted at the dark complexity of the man himself.

Though her brain noted changes—a tiny gold earring winking at her from his left ear, added lines of stress in his broad forehead, deeper grooves framing his hard mouth, a sharper edge to the cynicism in his eyes—she smiled at the memory of those lips brushing hers on that first magical night when she'd started falling in love.

"Hello, Prudy. Nice to see you again." His voice was cool, his gaze impersonal, before it dropped to the child in her arms, and Prudy felt a stab of pain.

"He looks like you, Uncle Case," Molly said, beaming down at her son.

"Poor kid," Case all but growled. "Maybe he'll get over it."

Molly punched him, and he grinned at her, revealing a flash of deep male dimples.

Remember the arguments and the anger, Prudy reminded herself as she inhaled the familiar scent of his after-shave. Remember the loneliness after he left, and the hours spent waiting by the phone. Squaring her shoulders, she lifted her chin and forced calm into her expression. When she met Case's gaze, he lifted one black eyebrow in a mocking salute.

*Bastard,* she thought, her temper sparking.

"If you'll take your places around the font, we'll begin," the pastor ordered with a brisk note of anticipation. "Godparents on my left, please. Parents on my right."

As Case took his place next to the woman he'd never figured to see again, he decided he needed a stiff drink. At least a double. Hell, no, a triple, he amended as the minister opened a small black book and cleared his throat.

Late afternoon sunshine spilled from the triangular window in the soaring facade behind the altar to bathe Prudy in a golden glow, and for an instant he felt his breath dam up in his throat. Her heart-shaped face was radiant beneath the coppery halo of her hair as she gazed down at the baby cradled in her arms. A shaft of pain shot through him, slicing neatly and efficiently through the chains he'd put around his emotions.

She looked so right, standing there. So serenely happy. Only someone who knew her very well, or loved her with all his heart, would notice the subtle curve of sadness at the corners of her smile.

He told himself he was neither—just a cop trained to notice the tiniest details. Like the fact that her profile was as fragile as ever, a heart-tugging combination of sensitive slopes and impish curves. It was a pixie's face, he'd teased her once. With lush brown eyes that took on a subtle gleam of golden warmth when she laughed and a wide expressive mouth. Pensive, sad, even trembling with anger, her mouth had once driven him crazy, just as her lush shape had once robbed him of good sense.

She was thinner now, he noticed, but the curves under the clinging material of her dress were generous enough to excite a dead man to life. Her derriere was sweetly rounded beneath the graceful folds of her skirt, and her breasts filled the bodice to perfection. In spite of her short stature, she had a ripe figure, as perfect now as it had been the first time he'd coaxed her to bare it to him.

Gritting his teeth, he dragged in a lungful of air, then let it out slowly. Did God punish a man for lusting after his ex-wife in church? he wondered as the solemn words of the ancient rite rolled over him. Because, if he did, Case was pretty sure he'd just been sentenced to the fires of hell....

IN CELEBRATION OF MOTHER'S DAY, JOIN
SILHOUETTE THIS MAY AS WE BRING YOU

# a funny thing
## HAPPENED ON THE WAY TO THE
# DELIVERY ROOM

THESE THREE STORIES, CELEBRATING THE
LIGHTER SIDE OF MOTHERHOOD, ARE
WRITTEN BY YOUR FAVORITE AUTHORS:

## KASEY MICHAELS
## KATHLEEN EAGLE
## EMILIE RICHARDS

When three couples make the trip to the delivery
room, they get more than their own bundles of
joy...they get the promise of love!

Available this May,
wherever Silhouette books are sold.

*Silhouette*®
TM

# Take 4 bestselling love stories FREE

## Plus get a FREE surprise gift!

## Special Limited-time Offer

**Mail to Silhouette Reader Service™**

**3010 Walden Avenue**
**P.O. Box 1867**
**Buffalo, N.Y. 14240-1867**

**YES!** Please send me 4 free Silhouette Desire® novels and my free surprise gift. Then send me 6 brand-new novels every month, which I will receive months before they appear in bookstores. Bill me at the low price of $2.90 each plus 25¢ delivery and applicable sales tax, if any.* That's the complete price and a savings of over 10% off the cover prices—quite a bargain! I understand that accepting the books and gift places me under no obligation ever to buy any books. I can always return a shipment and cancel at any time. Even if I never buy another book from Silhouette, the 4 free books and the surprise gift are mine to keep forever.

225 BPA A3UU

| | |
|---|---|
| Name | (PLEASE PRINT) |
| Address | Apt. No. |
| City | State | Zip |

This offer is limited to one order per household and not valid to present Silhouette Desire® subscribers. *Terms and prices are subject to change without notice.
Sales tax applicable in N.Y.

UDES-696 ©1990 Harlequin Enterprises Limited

# And the Winner Is...
# You!

...when you pick up these great titles
from our new promotion at your
favorite retail outlet this June!

## Diana Palmer
*The Case of the Mesmerizing Boss*

## Betty Neels
*The Convenient Wife*

## Annette Broadrick
*Irresistible*

## Emma Darcy
*A Wedding to Remember*

## Rachel Lee
*Lost Warriors*

## Marie Ferrarella
*Father Goose*

Look us up on-line at: http://www.romance.net          ATWI397-R

# As seen on TV!
# *Free Gift Offer*

With a Free Gift proof-of-purchase from any Silhouette® book, you can receive a beautiful cubic zirconia pendant.

This gorgeous marquise-shaped stone is a genuine cubic zirconia—accented by an 18" gold tone necklace.

(Approximate retail value $19.95)

# Send for yours today...
## compliments of ▼ *Silhouette*®

To receive your free gift, a cubic zirconia pendant, send us one original proof-of-purchase, photocopies not accepted, from the back of any Silhouette Romance™, Silhouette Desire®, Silhouette Special Edition®, Silhouette Intimate Moments® or Silhouette Yours Truly™ title available in February, March and April at your favorite retail outlet, together with the Free Gift Certificate, plus a check or money order for $1.65 U.S./$2.15 CAN. (do not send cash) to cover postage and handling, payable to Silhouette Free Gift Offer. We will send you the specified gift. Allow 6 to 8 weeks for delivery. Offer good until April 30, 1997 or while quantities last. Offer valid in the U.S. and Canada only.

## *Free Gift Certificate*

Name: _____

Address: _____

City: _____ State/Province: _____ Zip/Postal Code: _____

Mail this certificate, one proof-of-purchase and a check or money order for postage and handling to: SILHOUETTE FREE GIFT OFFER 1997. In the U.S.: 3010 Walden Avenue, P.O. Box 9077, Buffalo NY 14269-9077. In Canada: P.O. Box 613, Fort Erie, Ontario L2Z 5X3.

---

## FREE GIFT OFFER                                084-KFD
ONE PROOF-OF-PURCHASE
To collect your fabulous FREE GIFT, a cubic zirconia pendant, you must include this original proof-of-purchase for each gift with the properly completed Free Gift Certificate.

---

084-KFD

**This summer, the legend
continues in Jacobsville**

*Diana
Palmer*

## A LONG, TALL
## TEXAN SUMMER

**Three BRAND-NEW short stories**

This summer, Silhouette brings readers a special
collection for Diana Palmer's LONG, TALL TEXANS
fans. Diana has rounded up three **BRAND-NEW**
stories of love Texas-style, all set in Jacobsville,
Texas. Featuring the men you've grown to love from
this wonderful town, this collection is a must-have
for all fans!

*They grow 'em tall in the saddle in Texas—and
they've got love and marriage on their minds!*

Don't miss this collection of original Long, Tall Texans
stories...available in June at your favorite retail outlet.

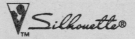